Tess Palmer's father had been a judge known the length and breadth of the northwest country for his fairness and his respect for justice. And he had inculcated these attributes in his daughter. Therefore she was greatly perturbed by a visit to a courtroom where one man was being sentenced to ten years for a petty theft, while a former judge who had stolen sizable amounts from public funds was given a suspended sentence.

Inasmuch as Tess' fiancé Matt Seares was involved as a lawyer in both cases, Tess turned to him for understanding—and received only cynical indifference.

In an excess of disillusionment, Tess set out to find a place in the mountains where she could temporarily be removed from her fellow men and regain her perspective. By chance, she reached Phantom Peak just as the Rangers were looking for a woman to man their fire station. So she settled on the mountain and became a lady lookout.

LADY LOOKOUT
OF PHANTOM PEAK

LADY LOOKOUT
OF
PHANTOM PEAK

by

BETTY BLOCKLINGER

PRESTIGE BOOKS
NEW YORK, NEW YORK

Prestige Books, Inc.
18 East 41st Street, New York, New York 10017

Printed in the United States of America

LADY LOOKOUT
OF PHANTOM PEAK

CHAPTER 1

A white blaze of early spring sunshine filled the courtroom. Irritably Tess wondered why the bailiff didn't order the blinds drawn or the awnings dropped. This room where her father, the late Judge Paulus Palmer, had presided so many years, could no longer stand such a penetrating light.

Two sentences had been handed down that morning. Early when court first convened, Decker Monrove had been brought in, his manacled hands held stiffly out in a gesture as defiant as the upthrust of his chin. Memory supplied her with pictures of Decker standing before the football coach, the senior class, the high school principal with that same defiance. Only a few had seen the bewildered misery in his eyes.

"Ten years."

The sentence was just. The value of the food he'd stolen from a grocery store amounted to less than forty dollars, but he'd carried a gun and had fired two shots. They'd been aimed at the grocer's feet. But another time the aim could be higher.

Matt Seares, his attorney, had made a dramatic plea on the final day of the trial. Decker had been in service. On his return he hadn't worked at his job long enough to be eligible for unemployment benefits before the logging outfit closed down. That was the year when a minimum of loggers could find work.

Decker had married in high school. There were children to be fed. Decker's mother had reared her brood of children on county relief funds. Tess could understand his revolt, his bitterness. Now he could either cool that revolt behind penitentiary walls or build it into habitual defiance.

Laws were made to protect grocers and others from guns carried by Deckers, as well as to punish the Deckers. Tess could accept that sentence as just, according to law.

It was the second one, just pronounced, which had thrown her mind into confusion.

Where Decker had stood alone, this defendant was surrounded by friends and family. His two attorneys, one of them Matt Seares, stood by proudly accepting the congratulations of all.

This defendant had stolen thousands of dollars from public funds; not forty dollars for food, but thousands of dollars for gambling.

He, who had once meted out justice from a lower bench, had violated his oath of office and his trust. And he had been given a suspended sentence.

Tess wondered, then stiffened. Matt Seares was excusing himself from the congratulators and stood looking at her. He would be over in a moment, and she wasn't ready to talk to him.

Matt, in the parlance of the day, was "going places." Handsome, quick-witted, enterprising; his name was already well known in the higher echelons of his political party.

I wonder, Tess thought as he moved past detaining hands, whether he's interested in me as a person or as the daughter of Judge Palmer, the 'old judge' held in such esteem all over the north-west?

"Tess girl," he beamed down on her, "we made it."

He waited a moment, and when she offered no congratulations he questioned her.

"Is it stealing with a gun in hand that makes the difference?" she asked soberly.

"Oh, now, darling, you, the old judge's daughter, ask that? It's intent."

"You mean this ex-Judge Juxton who's been stealing public funds for nearly a year didn't intend to steal?"

"Look, honey, this is no time to go into that. We'll have lunch and I'll try to explain the fine points. And I want to talk to you about us. Now these two trials are over, we—"

"Seares!"

Matt turned as his senior partner signaled, then turned back. "Meet me at the club at one o'clock. We'll lay our plans. Yes, coming," he broke off to say.

Tess felt her cheeks flaming until they matched the copper red of her hair. She felt like a volume of Blackstone pulled from a shelf, leafed through and thrust back to be studied at Matt's leisure.

In another moment she had wheeled out of the courtroom, hurried along the corridor and was racing down the steep granite stairway, giving thanks every step of the way that this was her day off from her stenographic duties at City Hall.

Once in her car, she hurried toward her home, but, when she reached the entrance to the grounds, she slowed down. The tree-studded lawns were in dire need of cutting; the big two and a half story house in need of paint. Why had Matt been so insistent she not sell?

"I've got to get away," she said aloud, and backed to turn toward the highway. "I've got to get clear away so I can see things from an impersonal perspective."

Thoughts raced along with the spinning car wheels. Matt had said they didn't build houses like hers these days, and she'd said, "Thank heaven. After Dad and I were alone we never used more than the first floor, and only part of that."

He'd said it was a wonderful place in which to entertain, and it had been. His grandfather had told him how he, as a small boy, had watched carriages drive up to discharge beautifully dressed ladies, and gentlemen in top hats. And Tess had thought of the necessities she was doing without merely to pay taxes and insurance and keep on one old servant so she wouldn't be alone in the empty rooms too much.

She swung onto the highway and turned south. Maybe Matt intended to marry her; maybe, as some said, he even now had an eye on the Governor's chair and needed a residence like hers.

"And just what makes him think I'd marry him?" she demanded of a truck driver who'd peered out of the cab curiously as he passed her.

I must be driving erratically, she thought. Better get off on a side road. Which way should she go? Which way? Two sides. Her father had said there were more than two sides to a question. There were as many as there were slopes on a mountain, and the only way to see the whole was to get above it, to reach a pinnacle.

On a rise, she looked east. The Cascades rose like a solid pale blue wall. To the west the Coast Range.

I'd like to climb to the top of one and pull the

sides up after me, she thought rebelliously.

Tess eased into the slow traffic lane, seeking a southwest side road. Some place in that jumble of mountains was a peak called Phantom that appeared and disappeared. Common sense told one it was the terrain, that this high shoulder sat at an angle from its neighbors, and light bringing them into deep color didn't strike its granite sides. Then too, it was slightly above timberline, gray as the sky while surrounding mountains were deep blue-green with timber.

If I could reach that I could disappear with it, she thought.

Dimly she was aware of the beauty in the foreground. Wild roses tumbled along fence lines foaming in pink and white. Wild flags of lavender-blue were matted at their feet.

She slowed as a flock of wild canaries came in to land in small black yellow balls before her. Seeking dust, she imagined, and sounded her horn.

Bobolinks caroled defiance at the sound, and Tess, starting up again, wondered what was wrong with the world. With so much beauty, how could it hold corruption too?

As she entered the foothills, Scotch broom lined the road in massed golden bloom and spread copper patches on hillside glades. How long had it been since she'd watched the spring parade? And why hadn't she?

She'd been too encased in her own small world. When any of her crowd went out, they chose main highways, their eyes intent upon speedometers and their thoughts on how quickly they could reach their destination—other small worlds as static as their own.

I'll sell the house, she thought, and build a cabin out here. I'll line the walls with books; that set of John Burroughs Dad used to read from. I'll look at life through the eyes of a naturalist and forget crime and justice and the lack of it.

A young river appeared by the roadside, and she thought she'd like to build beside that, watching dappled sun and shadow in the day-time and hearing the trout jump at twilight. And then she remembered that rivers had a way of rising and engulfing cabins in the winter.

Mountain top or nothing, she decided, for where else could she keep Matt from engulfing her in persuasive arguments. And if she, like a jury, ever succumbed to them she'd be like that cabin she'd envisioned, swept away into depths she couldn't fathom.

The idea of living on a mountain top, alone, was so ludicrous she laughed a little. Maybe she was merely hungry. She'd pull into that little logging town ahead. Coffee and a sandwich, and perhaps even Matt would put me into focus, she thought.

Snaking in between two trucks towering with logs, she went into the small café and found truckers there, teasing a waitress. The atmosphere was refreshing. Here no one was trying to pretend to be anything but what they were.

Driving on, refreshed herself, she wondered why her friends desired to be more than they were: richer, more socially acceptable and more important. Why? Could any mountain top give her all sides to that question?

District fire warden Bill Mondy, making a final check of a new road into a timber stand of the Willoughby Lumber company, stopped at his station wagon door to look around. The sudden unseasonable heat which had clamped down on the northwest was rapidly sucking up protective moisture. If it kept up, one violent electric storm could set off a rash of small fires.

Already he'd opened two of the higher lookout stations; central lookout on Speiler Mountain went up first. However, with 700,000 acres of timber to guard against freak weather, more lookouts would be needed soon. The housewives who manned the majority of the lookouts would be available, but the schoolteachers still had six weeks of school ahead of them.

Al King, member of his fire suppression crew, sensing the warden's thoughts, asked, "Anyone for Phantom Peak yet?"

"No. Mrs. Paul gave us her final word only yesterday. I told her to go on and enjoy her lucky break; we had plenty of applicants. Headquarters received five hundred applications after that story came out in a national magazine. Even had long distance calls from other states."

They got into the station wagon and started down.

Al gave his chief a commiserative look. Those few grey hairs, he believed, had come when Mondy had waited in the valley, wondering if his lookouts were on duty, taking a nap, lost in a book, or even day-dreaming.

They had their hourly check-in by central lookout, but an awful lot could happen in an hour. A reported smoke could be reached by the suppression crew; a "sleeper" awakened by a fresh breeze could run up a dry branch, heralding its danger. Time was an all-important element in fire suppression, and in the extreme fire danger period, constant watch was needed.

Al thought of the girls who had come to him asking for an introduction to the warden. To most of them a lookout job was a romantic way of spending a vacation with pay.

He wondered how many had ever spent a night alone even in the city and how long they'd last on a lonely peak with nothing but the stars and weirdly whispering winds for company; how long they'd last with gale winds buffeting their tower, thunder shaking it and jagged lightning streaking around their seemingly fragile shelter.

"I had thought of Mrs. Dannish," Mondy said, "but I'm not sure of her heart."

Al nodded. Climbing a sixty or one-hundred

foot stairway at high altitudes took a stout heart. There was another reason for hourly check-ins with central lookout. When central lookout received no check from her call to another lookout, she alerted the dispatcher at district Headquarters and he saw to it that someone was sent up to investigate immediately.

It took a lot of screening to choose the right person for a lookout. Health, sense of responsibility, steady nerves, quick reflexes and above all, perhaps, the ability to remain alone day and night; sometimes, when the crews were intent upon a fire, for longer periods of time.

Coming out of the timber, and entering the road skirting a canyon, Mondy slowed.

"Over there at the Ranson gate—a girl. Now what's she doing up here?"

"Probably off on the wrong road."

"She can read the 'No Trespassing' signs, but she's trying to open the gate. Can't she see it's padlocked?"

"It isn't a place I'd choose to turn around, and you know how women are about backing. That's a dangerous and crooked road behind her."

"Better check." And the station wagon sped on.

When they came to a turn on the other road, they stopped. Ahead they could see the car backing steadily. There was no hesitation, no clinging to the inner side. She might have been backing out of a driveway and not down a mountain road with a chasm on one side. Obviously, a girl who didn't lose her head.

"There should be a sign," Tess announced, stopping beside the station wagon.

"There was this morning," Mondy told her. "Some truck must have sideswiped it. But if you're heading for the coast—"

"There is nothing I want less," Tess broke in to say. "It's matted with people. Or haven't you ever been so sick of people you wanted to find a high mountain and pull up the sides?"

"Quarrel with the boy friend?" Al asked.

Tess whirled on him. "No, with the world." Then, seeing the suspicious alarm on their faces: "I'm not contemplating suicide, or faking a lost woman in order to break into headlines. This morning in a courtroom where my father sat for years, I heard a sentence sending a man to the penitentiary for stealing groceries; another man, who'd stolen thousands in public funds, was given probation.

"I thought if there was a road near Phantom Peak, I could get high enough to view the picture as a whole; see how our youth can respect laws that show such partiality."

King moved abruptly, and Mondy looked at him. "Think you could show Miss Palmer? You have the lookout gear in your truck. You might take her up with you."

CHAPTER 2

Al King looked at the warden in surprise, said, "Of course; meet you at Milltown," and got back into the station wagon.

"The girl," Mondy told him when they were under way, "is obviously the daughter of Judge Paulus Palmer who died on the bench a little over a year ago. Maybe you remember?"

King nodded. "Remember reading about it."

"He was as just as they come, and a stickler for the law as it is written. If the President had been given a traffic ticket, he'd have imposed a fine as quickly as though he'd been a teen-ager.

"A girl brought up in that atmosphere would be upset by the Juxton and Monrove sentences this morning. I imagine she knew both defendants."

"Oh, that was on the news broadcast we listened to. That Monrove was a young fellow. You don't think—"

"I don't." Mondy was definite. "Besides, Monrove was married."

"I appreciate having company on the trip," King told him. "But how about that answer I'm supposed to give?"

"I think you have it. You spent two college vacations in a lookout, didn't you? And you've been with fire suppression three years. What's the greatest danger to a forest as a whole?"

Al considered this for a few minutes, then snapped his fingers. "Got it," he replied. "From Phantom I can really illustrate."

Tess drove down to the mill town, not too pleased with the way her trip had turned out. She had been seeking solitude. Now she was literally stuck with what she assumed was a guard. Why else would the warden have suggested she be taken in some truck rather than follow in her own car?

When she was transferred to the forestry truck and they were under way, she was surprised at the direction they took.

"I'd have said Phantom Peak was that way," she remarked, pointing in another direction.

Al nodded. "Like not seeing the forest for the trees. If you're up against a low hill, you can't see how close you are to the mountain."

Tess really looked at him for the first time. He had none of Matt's good looks; the type sought for in motion picture and advertising photographs. His face was too long and, at this hour of the day, his ordinary brown hair was a bit lank. He looked, she thought, like any of a hundred other men one might meet on a college campus or a city street.

Exposed as she'd been to Matt's driving ambition, she wondered about him and sought to learn the answers by adroit questioning.

They were on the last rise. The peak was just ahead before she realized she had been the one to give information; that now this man knew a great deal about her and she little more about him than she'd known in the beginning.

"There's your peak," he remarked, slowing the truck. "Quite a chunk."

It was quite a chunk of rock and earth, fringed round by wind-slanted trees and topped by what looked like a long-legged insect wearing a square hat.

It wasn't at all what she'd expected.

"Disappointed?"

"Oh, no. I thought it would be surrounded by sharp cliffs."

"There's one on the north side that gave it the name Phantom. Its color merges into the color of the sky at times."

They drove into the darkness of a canyon; then the truck in its lowest gear began a sharp ascent to wind in S curves, rising toward increasing light and coming out into the full strong sunlight as they neared the lookout.

"Try not to look until you're up on the catwalk," King advised, and obediently Tess kept her range of vision to nearby objects.

And then, when they had left the truck and were climbing a stairway which went up in sections one hundred feet into the air, Tess felt she was climbing a cobweb.

She paused to wait as King worked with a trap door, then stepped up into darkness.

"Shutters are down," he explained. "Here." And he extended a hand, leading her across to a door also barred against winter storms.

"Does height bother you?" he asked, then remembered the way she had backed down the narrow canyon road.

"Not at all," she began, stepping out. Or did it? Was it height, or was it seeing so much of the world suddenly spread out at her feet?

"It's better than flying," she insisted breathlessly. "The world remains static so you can actually look at it. It's stupendous!"

Mt. Hood, Mt. Jefferson, the Sisters and St. Helens stood up like golden sentinels. And below, like a many patterned quilt ruffled on the edges with hills, the valley lay in squares; squares of woods, lots, grain fields, towns.

King led her around the catwalk which skirted the cabin-like room. To the south and west she saw mountains, a veritable sea of mountains; each rose like a wave, dark at its base, glowing with sunset on the ridge.

"And peopled with trees." She switched metaphors quickly, remembering someone saying Oregon timberlands were all logged off.

"The state still has one fourth of the forests of the nation," King said, intent upon lifting a shutter which would form both a shade for the walk and the inner room. "Quite a responsibility to protect them," he continued.

King, watching her expression, decided this was the time to relay Mondy's message.

"You said the hills were peopled with trees. From up here you get a picture of the whole. You may have a fair idea of what the state and federal foresters do to protect these trees.

"Which would you consider of more ultimate danger, a quick fire, seen immediately, or one that smoldered in the duff, the residue of half decayed stuff that carpets forests?"

"I suppose the smoldering one," Tess returned after a moment's thought. "It could work along in different directions, sort of get its preliminary work over with before breaking out."

"—And because it wasn't seen in the beginning be that much harder to suppress. All right; now switch that thought to those sentences this morning. I don't know how you feel about the chap who robbed the grocer—"

"That's too deep to go into now," she hurried to say, "but I was more disturbed at the comparative sentences, the lack of justice in the second case."

"A lot of people are going to feel that way. The news of it will be the quick bright fire spurring the voters to action. And it may squelch a lot of sleepers. Remember people get the kind of government they deserve."

But Tess was only partly comforted. "I think," she ventured, "that what we need politically is a series of fire lookouts, people in high places, like the Senate Investigating Committee."

King nodded. "That committee wasn't as fortunate as the Department of Forestry. It lacked the suppression crews trained to act with authority. But that's up to us, our generation.

"How many of your friends bother to vote or, voting, take time beforehand to study the men and the issues?"

Tess admitted there weren't many. Most of them voted by emotional reaction. Others were too busy having fun or building careers that would give them prominence and above all—wealth.

"Like so-called sportsmen who want the forests to provide them with good hunting, yet neglect to put out fires that can destroy the forest and the game. Wealth and importance won't be of any use if they haven't any place to display them."

He was around the cabin now. The shutters were up; their green interiors provided relief from the glare that would distract the eyes of a person on duty, and shelter from rain.

Tess followed him in and looked around with interest. In one corner was a comfortable-looking couch, in another a small stove for cooking and beneath it a heater, both equipped for bottled gas. There were book racks and, of all things, a clothes press lying on its side, the top on a level with the window. She noticed a table, two chairs and an easy chair.

It was the fire-finder in the center of the cabin that dominated the room. At easy reading height, it held a map of the district, and an alidade, which to her merely looked like a weird object but which she supposed moved around to provide the exact spot a fire was located.

King went down to the truck and Tess, alone, went back to the catwalk. She looked down on the valley side, then around, and at the wilderness of the coast range.

For a moment she had what she'd been seeking all day—solitude. If she were to go in and close that trap door, she would be in an inaccessible place.

Imagine being in a place completely alone and safe; stars at night and sun in the daytime her only companions.

She heard King come up and for a moment said nothing. Then she saw far to the west a bright red splash and called.

"Reflection of the sun on the water. Or didn't you realize that was the Pacific out there?"

"I *am* stupid," she confessed, "but things look different up here."

"There was a haze there when you looked before, so don't blame yourself. You should hear some of the things the lookouts report as fires before they've become acquainted with their area."

"And these live on as jokes, I suppose?"

"Only to them. It's better to report the spray of a waterfall as smoke than miss real smoke. Well, ready to leave?"

She wasn't. She walked back around the cabin and looked out to the east.

"Why, it's almost twilight down there," she cried. And in another moment, "Darkness doesn't descend, does it? It rises like purple dye.

"Oh, I wish I could stay. Couldn't I? Just for one night?"

"You mean you wouldn't be afraid?"

"I'm used to being alone in a big house. This isn't one tenth as dangerous as that."

"But you're accustomed to that particular house." And finding that made no impression he said, "Besides, you've no food or water."

She looked around then. "What do the look-outs do for water? Oh, I remember reading they go to some nearby spring if there isn't clean snow to melt."

"Not here. We truck it up; then it's hoisted up by windless to the cabin. Of course anyone wanting to do any extensive washing—"

"And it's too late for you to take me back for my car and let me return."

"I couldn't," he said flatly. "This isn't exactly—"

"A tourist cabin," she finished for him. "All

right, I should be grateful to you for bringing me up here at all."

She said nothing more until they were walking toward the truck. Then she ventured, "I suppose I could come back up here alone another day."

He said the roads were private, the land in the area owned by lumber companies and open to the public only during certain seasons for hunting or fishing.

And then abruptly he asked, "Are you trying to run to mountain tops or run away from something else?"

"Both," she replied thoughtfully. "I'm running away, and chose a mountain top so I can really see what I think I must run away from; see if it is as fruitless as I think it is."

"There are other mountains with good highways, open to the public."

She smiled at him. "Remember, you said, 'Here's *your* mountain.' Out of a thousand miles of mountains, from border to border, this is the one I want."

"Women!" barked Al, and got into the truck.

They dipped into the darkness of the canyons, and the truck headlights picked up trunks of trees in park-like formation.

"Ever been in a forest fire?" King asked.

"Once, when I was very small. My folks had quite a time with me afterwards. I'd been told trees were living things. Childlike, I assumed they were like animals, and when the fire struck I thought the sound they made was the agony they suffered. I imagined they were literally chained to the ground and burning to death. I've hated fires ever since."

Nearing the mill town, he suggested they stop for dinner and didn't tell her that the meal he usually took with the rest of the crew at district headquaters was well over.

Tess was delighted. She liked Al King well enough. But she thought of him more as the man who'd taken her to her chosen mountain top than as an individual.

When they went into the café and Tess saw other girls turning for a second look, speaking shyly or eagerly and indulging in all of the little feminine acts of preening any woman recognizes, she turned to him in surprise.

"I must have been dull company," she apologized, "so immersed in my own troubles I haven't thought of anyone else."

Her second surprise came when he didn't deny it but merely looked at her, his eyes crinkled with amusement.

Because she'd been brought up by a father, she sought to make amends in the only way she knew: by talking of this man's chosen profession.

Why, she asked, was it necessary for a small crew to be maintained the year around, here in this rain country?

"What would you think of a nation that didn't prepare for action before the enemy was well into its territory?

"The district warden is like a general. He has to know where the enemy could strike; he has to know every foot of the terrain so he can get men and equipment into the line of action in the shortest time. To do this he has to know every accessible road and see that it's kept in condition."

He continued with the simile, and Tess, remembering the cabin atop the spiderweb stairway, capped it with, "And the lookouts are the sentries."

"More than that. They're human radar stations alerting the dispatcher at the first approach of the enemy."

Tess mused over the term enemy and finally asked why he had chosen his particular profession. She didn't say she knew he had capabilities which would have placed him in the other positions they'd discussed; positions of wealth and importance.

"I started out with a yen for ancient history that led me to archeology. I studied and read everything I could find, going back as far as there is a record of man. And then one day, out in eastern Oregon, I happened to visit the Lost Forest. You know the place, not lost in the sense of unable to find, but seemingly lost from its own kind. Only forests aren't transients; they don't pick up their roots and move to a new clime. That triggered me into studying other lands, and the Bible and its history.

"Everywhere I found traces of lands, now barren, that had once been forested. And I found in every legend, fire-spitting monsters of one type or another. These legends, I was convinced, were based upon lightning, fire from the sky striking and consuming.

"We think of the Sahara as a desert that has always been a waste of sands, yet Egyptian lore tells of the god Ptah throwing fire at a forest from his place in the sky.

"I began to study forests and what they mean to a country; how they hold the water from running off to the sea; how their roots keep the earth from being washed away; how the water table is maintained.

"To me the most important job in the world became one where I'd have a hand in holding those forest lands where they are, saving our land from erosion, keeping our water available for the use of man. So," he lifted his hands, "I switched to forestry."

Tess, who's listened, fascinated, remembered what he'd said about keeping land for use when they'd spoken of leniency in the administration of law. The lookout tower on Phantom Peak assumed another dimension.

"Mr. King," she leaned forward, "what would I have to do to become a lookout?"

CHAPTER 3

Al King, who felt himself cursed with a western Oregon complexion, kept clean by the moist Pacific winds, hadn't blushed since he'd left high school. Now his face was crimson.

"Oh, now look, Miss Palmer. I wasn't trying to sell you on forestry."

"I know," she spoke impatiently, "but don't you see how that would answer all of my problems? Now I'm doing work anyone can do. As a lookout I'd feel I was doing something really worth while. Now I'm sick of people and their pettiness. As a lookout I'd be dealing with bigger, impersonal values."

"I wonder if you'd feel those bigger things were impersonal if a lively electric storm chose your peak to put on a pyrotechnical party. Believe me, you have an idea every jagged streak has your name on it."

"You showed me how the cabins were insulated. I'd be safer than in my own home. Besides, what's more impersonal than some drunken driver ramming into the hereafter? The odds are far greater there."

"All right, but what about being there alone? Right now you think you'd like that. But a lookout spends a good three months up there, ninety days, without Saturday afternoons and Sundays off."

Tess gave him a radiant smile. "Imagine all of those blessed days without having to think up excuses for not attending something that bores me to tears. Besides, other girls and women man the lookouts."

"The average age in our Tyee district," he commented dryly, "is forty-five. There are some younger women; schoolteachers and occasionally a high school girl. The last one, seventeen, lasted two days."

"Why are you trying to discourage me?"

King thought of the stacks of letters at the

state office; of the pile of applications that came yearly to the district warden.

"I'm not, exactly. In the first place I have nothing to do with it, nothing to say about it. I just happen to know how many want the same thing. And this is late in the season; a dry season with hot weather calling for an electric storm. Actually, there are only two spots open, and one lookout isn't completed yet. The other is—" he stopped and looked miserable.

"Phantom Peak!" Tess cried triumphantly.

"Purely by accident. The woman who's had that for three years just won some contest that's giving her a trip to Japan. She has a son stationed there. But," he added, "Mondy has a woman ready to fill the spot."

Tess hadn't been reared by a judge without learning to weigh evidence. She smiled at King now. "If Mr. Mondy has someone ready to go in there, why did you say it was open?"

King sighed deeply. "I didn't want you disappointed. It is open. There isn't just one but a dozen who'd jump at the chance. They haven't been screened yet."

"Screened?"

"Down at headquarters, the warden and the dispatcher are quick at determining qualifications. They've had so many applicants, tried out so many. Qualifications aren't something found in written answers. I guess you'd call it temperament. It takes a certain temperament to make a good lookout, and it's important to the whole district that the right type is in every station."

To terminate the dangerous topic he rose, assisted her into her light topcoat and steered her out of the danger spot into the truck where traffic might give him some excuse for evading her questions. Besides, her car was only a mile away.

But he hated to see her drive away. She was different from any girl he'd ever met. And she would, he believed, make a fine lookout.

Heading back to district headquarters, he considered her final words. "Tell Mr. Mondy I'll be in Monday morning. I'm taking time off my job for that."

He'd warned her the warden was not in the office much, but she'd said she'd wait until he was there. From what he'd told her of the dispatcher, she'd learn all he had time to teach her as she waited.

King reported to Mondy the next morning and the warden heard him through with an amused twinkle.

"Too bad there are so many ahead of her," he remarked. "She'd make a fine lookout."

"How do you know?" King asked. "Why, you hardly saw her."

"A very determined young woman heading for a peak came up to a locked gate. She took in the situation, got back in her car and backed down. That little pantomime we saw revealed a lot. Acceptance of a situation without a show of temper; observance of the road she'd traveled, or she couldn't have backed down as she did; steady nerves.

"Another quality. She had a problem. Most people run to the nearest listener and talk it out. She was running away from listeners so she could think it out. A lookout hasn't a chance to talk things over; she has to think them out herself.

"How did you like her?"

King turned away quickly but not before Mondy had seen the sudden scarlet in his face.

This time the warden's shoulders moved a little convulsively, betraying his amusement.

"Incidentally," he called after him, "I won't be in Monday. Tom will talk to her." And Winston, who'd been sitting before the panel controlling the radio outlets of all stations in the district, looked up, the expression in his grey eyes as discomfiting to King, as the warden's.

Tess, getting into her car after having had dinner with Al, set off on her long drive, her mind filled with new thoughts. She hadn't been so happy since she'd left college. Then she had felt the world was definitely her oyster and all she'd have to do was pry a little and the top lid would flip up to disclose a pearl of particular beauty.

A few weeks at home and she'd realized her father's need of her. The housekeeper could take care of his physical needs, but he needed someone to whom he could talk freely. He had learned the bitter way that one holding political position couldn't risk or impose on outside friendship.

To fill the daytime hours, Tess had taken a short business course, found a routine position at City Hall, and become absorbed in the social life of her set. She hadn't been unhappy.

The death of Judge Palmer had changed everything. It had brought Matt Seares sharply into focus in her life. Until then he had been a busy young attorney she met occasionally at the home of friends, at social functions and consulting with her father.

After the death of the judge Matt had somehow stepped into the first role, advising her on many points she argued with the firm about settling the estate.

Actually there had been little to settle. The judge had given up most of his private practice, devoting full time to his official duties.

There was the big house centered in a parklike block. The city had wanted it for a library and museum, but Matt had advised against the sale. In the first place, he'd reasoned, they'd offered only half its value; in the second, its true value would be lost. It had been built and maintained as a home for four generations.

"I've seen the city architects' plans," he'd said. "It will look like a bastille, and before long they'll tear it down and put up some other nightmare. Let's try to hold on to some tradition."

Driving on, Tess considered the house. The estate had been settled four months ago. The city's offer still held.

I'll sell, she was thinking. Mr. King said the lookout pay was two hundred and something the first year. Even if the money for the house isn't released by fall, I can find another job. Stenographers always can.

An inner voice questioned, "And Matt?"

Well, she stepped on the accelerator, if Matt only wanted to marry the house—

The highway was not the place to go into that; she'd think about the lookout. Again the car picked up speed. The freedom of being high above interference, of being closed off from friends of her fathers who said do this and do that; all pulling in different directions.

It was nearly midnight when she turned into her driveway and wound up to the dark house.

Then into the glare of her headlights stepped the man she'd been thinking about.

"Where in the name of heaven have you been?" he demanded angrily. "You said you'd meet me at the club."

"No," Tess remained behind the wheel, "you

said I'd meet you there. And then you walked off, taking it for granted."

"You mean you were trying to punish me?" he asked incredulously.

"No," she returned thoughtfully, "I'm afraid I didn't think about you at all. I had other plans and I went about fulfilling them."

To a handsome young man with a future, accustomed to having every mother's daughter eager to snatch him, Tess could not have conjured up any words more devastating to his morale.

"Coming home at this hour of the night to this house alone?" he asked. "You, the judge's daughter?"

"Matt," she reproved, "you were the very one to tell me that any enemies Dad had would only try to harm him. Hurting me wouldn't harm him now. Besides, I'm too tired to argue."

"You're not too tired to listen to reason. I wanted to wait until fall, but someone has to look after you. We'd better be married right away."

She shouldn't have laughed. But when a girl has dreamed of the one great moment when a man will speak of marriage, and then it comes like this, angrily as though he were assuming some obligation, she has either to laugh or cry.

"I find nothing humorous in the idea," he remarked stiffly.

"Not in the idea," she conceded. "But, my goodness Matt, you make marrying me sound like a sentence."

"I didn't mean it that way, Tess, but I've been worried. In another half-hour I'd have raised someone at Salem to look up your car license number and alert the State Police. You've never acted this way before," he explained.

"I know. I've always been right where anyone could put their finger on me."

"I'll pick you up at one o'clock and we'll have dinner at the coast."

"And if I'm not here?"

For a moment he was exasperated; then the smile that won him friends and destroyed the weapons of would-be enemies was turned on Tess.

"Tess, will you have dinner with me tomorrow? I'd thought of the coast, but if you've some place else you prefer, we can go there. And, Tess, forgive me for being so abrupt. I've got so much on my mind these days."

Gravely she nodded. "At one. And, Matt, you don't have to come in. Jim Gavin is on this beat, and if there was any suspicious characters within blocks Jim would have had him in the city jail hours ago."

He waited until her lights were on, until living room and hall lights went off, and tried to wait until the soft glow of the bed lamp died, but that remained on so long he decided she must be reading.

But Tess wasn't reading. She was sitting up in bed with a pad and pencil jotting down hurried notes. There was so little she wanted to keep for herself: her father's favorite chair, the books she had moved from the library to her small suite.

For a moment she thought of Matt and his feeling about the big house. Could houses make men? Perhaps somewhere in his mind there was the feeling that by living here, he could more readily represent the law as it was written and meant.

Oh, rubbish, she sighed, whoever heard of that as a reason? Now what clothes will I need? How few can I get along with?

An hour passed, and then the light went out and sleepily Tess asked the final question. And what on earth makes me think I can have that lookout, with a whole list of applicants ahead of me?

She awakened next morning feeling dull and depressed.

Straightening up her room, she found the list she had made the night before, and sharp memory of the lookout on Phantom Peak returned.

I don't have to stay on here, she reasoned. I can still sell and escape.

Matt arrived at one-thirty, apologizing for the delay. "I know," Tess soothed him. "You ran into some men and got to talking."

"As a matter of fact, I did," he returned, then absently patted the ornate portals of the big door. "Ready? Wonderful old house," he commented as they went down the stairway.

"I should be as foursquare and solid," Tess muttered, and wondered, if they ever married and he were to carry her over the threshold, if he'd kiss the great oaken door and forget the bride.

"I didn't hear you."

"It's just as well." And Matt was so preoccupied he hadn't realized what that could mean.

Driving north instead of west, Matt explained he'd decided the coast would be too crowded on such a beautiful day. He wanted a quiet spot where they could talk.

Later, when they reached the outskirts of Portland and turned into a boulevard rising along the western hills, she felt he was taking an unfair advantage. They would come to a beautiful spot with café windows, and a view of the river and city below, and snow-capped mountains north and east.

It was here he had brought her that first Sunday after her father's death and somehow removed her dreadful feeling of loneliness. He had proven then that he was capable of great tenderness.

They said little during dinner. Matt asked if she'd had a nice time the previous day and she assured him she had had a wonderful time.

"I went away to think things out," she added.

"Wasn't that rather foolish, Tess?" he reproved. "I'd have explained it to you. You know as well as I that Decker's a potential criminal, a killer, while Juxton, given a chance, will make restitution, which is more than he could do behind bars."

He'd missed the point, Tess thought.

"One thing yesterday taught me," Matt went on, "was the necessity of having you where I could find you. I went into action this morning."

Tess turned from contemplation of Mt. St. Helens, a perfect cone of snow on grape blue foothills, and listened in consternation.

"Decorators should be able to have the house ready by the last day of June. We'll need all the guest rooms; want to ask quite a few from Salem, Medford and three from Eastern Oregon.

"You'll have nothing to worry about. I talked to Smithie this morning. He said you were a good stenographer, but because of the nature of your work could be replaced at any time, so I quit for you. Now you can go about getting your trousseau.

"Mrs. Ranford will be glad to take over the chaperoning. You can move in with them any time, and she can head the reception committee, manage the house and the guests. She's accustomed to that, you know, after all those years at the capitol."

Tess listened in stupified silence. She listened right up to the moment Matt deposited her at her own door; then she shook her head. She didn't want him to come in.

"Thank you for giving my notice to Smithie," she said. "I intended to do it tomorrow morning. And, Matt, cancel any other plans."

"Tess, what's wrong, girl? We're going to be married, remember?"

"Matt," she had the key in the lock and turned, her hand on the doorknob. "You don't want to marry me; you want to marry this house."

He made a few protests, but she shook her head. "Do you think I want a husband who looks upon me as something that was thrown in with the house? A piece of furniture, a newel, or a rock in the foundation?

"Find yourself some other house to love. I sold this to the city this morning."

CHAPTER 4

Watching Matt, Tess felt sorry for him. The Palmer house had been a symbol of success to him and he'd seen it abruptly snatched away, placed beyond his reach. But her pity was impersonal.

At length he asked if she thought she'd treated him fairly.

"I don't know, Matt," she answered. "There is so much I don't know. Talking it over with others doesn't help. These are things I have to think out for myself. Good night."

Tess leaned against the door a moment, listening to Matt knock and then to the ringing of the door chimes. She hurried to the telephone to call her father's former law partner, whom he'd named administrator.

"Uncle Dean, I meant what I said this morning. I want to make sure that sale goes through. How far can you go without my signature?"

Near midnight, bags in her car, she drove to Dean Matson's home and was let into his study.

"I want to make sure this isn't an emotional reaction to some lovers' quarrel," he said severely. "Matt telephoned me."

"Lovers?" Tess laughed. "Uncle Dean, love is the one thing Matt hasn't thought necessary for marriage."

As she talked she told more than she realized. "I'm so tired of living in a mausoleum. I want a home, not a show place."

"You realize this can mean the breaking of your engagement to Matt."

"Oh, but we've never been engaged. Matt has never asked me if I would marry him. He just went ahead and planned the wedding."

"Hmm," mused Matson, and pulled some papers forward. "I understand now what you meant about young Matt marrying the house.

Wouldn't be surprised if you were being wise in this. Of course you've made other plans."

She said she had. She also knew she would receive less from the city than from a possible sale to some other buyer and that she would not be receiving any money from the sale for some time.

Just after midnight Mrs. Matson ushered in two men whom Tess knew, and explained to them that Miss Palmer had a business appointment early the next morning in a city some distance away. She wanted the sale under way before she left. As it was now officially Monday, the papers drawn up would be bonafide.

Tess left immediately, drove once around the house and saw it standing tall and gaunt and forbidding. Then she drove on out of town.

She'd have to return to dispose of furniture, pack personal belongings and close out small business matters, but actually she had taken her real farewell. Her decision was made.

It wasn't a happy leave-taking. Memories of Matt when she'd first know him kept intruding and with them a sense of guilt, of having done some irreparable damage to another.

She had thought she loved him. In the beginning he had been attentive; then came the party's time for choosing candidates for the primaries, and Matt's increasing law practice. At first dates were broken with apologies, then sometimes forgotten altogether.

Mrs. Ranford, present at one of the latter, had treated it lightly. "It's the price a girl pays for having been chosen by a man who cares about the world they live in."

In a motel Tess tossed restlessly and remembered the boy who had broken a date and what her father had said. "There'll always be pressures to keep a boy like that from keeping his dates with you."

Well, now she'd know. She'd removed the house that stood between them and in a sense, with it, her position as Judge Palmer's daughter. From now on she'd be just any girl working for a living. Would Matt be able to see the forest in spite of the trees?

Morning brought grim determination. For the first time in her life she was completely on her own. If she didn't win the lookout post she would be looking for work as any other girl. No longer would her way be smoothed by her father's reputation.

It was shortly after eight o'clock when she drove into Forestville, stopping at the outskirts to study the big fire hazard meter placed where the roads forked.

It resembled plates of cake she'd seen at church socials; triangles of pistachio, strawberry, peach and lemon icing. An indicator could be moved to show lumber men, loggers, hunters and fishermen, and the prevailing conditions in the woods—low, moderate, high or extreme.

Extreme, she remembered, is when even a spark from the backfire of a truck can set off a fire; that's when everyone but foresters are supposed to stay out of the danger zone.

Through the mill district Tess drove, dodging huge trailers of lumber, making way for empty logging trucks barreling back to the timber, and then into a quiet residential district.

After the first stop sign on the right-hand

road, Al King had said, and soon she saw a big sign—Tyee Fire District Headquarters.

When she drove up to the small colony of forest green buildings Tess had her first sharp moment of uncertainty. She pretended she was still sitting in the car to make a survey of the buildings. The large one to the left was of course for equipment, the one directly ahead, administration; but what were the others?

"Oh, get on with it," she whispered, and was out of the car and up the short walk before she had time to think of other reasons to delay.

The reception room was empty, but through a window she could see someone sitting before a panel of a short wave radio set. A voice sounded with a peculiar, abrupt squawk. He answered, then got up and came in to stand on the opposite side of the high counter.

"I," began Tess, "am Tess Palmer."

"Yes, Miss Palmer?"

Tess thought this grey-haired man had the kindest eyes she'd ever seen, and abruptly and breathlessly she said, "And I'm scared to death."

"Now why would anything here frighten you?"

"It isn't that. It's because I've never wanted anything as much as a lookout, particularly the Phantom Peak lookout station. Mr. King took me up there Saturday."

"And this is Monday. When you went up you were not thinking of the lookout. You haven't taken much time to think it over, have you, Miss Palmer?"

"An awful lot can happen in a short time, Mr.—"

"Winston. You've discussed this with your family?"

"I haven't any family, just an administrator, and he's known me so long he knows I don't jump off deep ends. That sounds as though I didn't need work, but I do."

"You know the pay a lookout receives? Two hundred and twenty-two a month the first year, then fifteen dollars more each season until the maximum of two eighty."

She smiled. "At least none of that would be going out in rent. And I'm a fair stenographer. I should be able to find winter work."

He suggested she come into his office, gravely indicating she should sit in his chair, and when she did the chair tipped back and arms and legs flew out in windmill fashion.

"It won't go over," he assured her.

It was a wonderful ice-breaker. Tess found her fear had vanished; her tense nerves had relaxed. Now she could really talk to him.

Adroitly he questioned her; led her to reveal her basic characteristics. Just as the warden was dependent upon his lookout sentinels to report the areas where he would deploy his fighters, so was this dispatcher dependent upon their calmness and their accuracy in times of stress.

Tess learned he would sit before that big radio all day and, during extreme hazard or a fire, all night as well, taking calls, sending calls, co-ordinating information; literally manipulating the distant field from this center.

And Phantom was an important peak. Because of the sharp drop to the north, the lookout had view of a danger area, a hunters' paradise. And not all hunters were sports-men. Fishermen too played the stream during steel-head season. And in years like this, they could pose a hazard.

When they were through he told her the

woman they'd expected to take the lookout had had a physical check-up and her physician had said it wasn't advisable. There were one or two others with applications in who had to be interviewed; however, and if Miss Palmer had the time, he'd advise her to attend the three day Guard School.

"We have two new sessions going this year. One has been completed; the other will be by mid-season. The first has been filled; you might be eligible for the second."

"At least I'd be ready," she agreed.

She was to return in two days. Driving off, she considered how to use those days. She didn't want to return home until she had a definite plan.

Driving on to the state capitol, she found a motel, checked the list she'd drawn up and went shopping for that now elusive object, a kerosene lamp. What she would do with it if she didn't win a lookout, she didn't know.

Books were next, and across from the post office she found a second-hand bookstore offering much of what she wanted—Indian lore, adventure stories about men of earlier generations who

had trod the mountains on which she would look
down, histories of pioneers of that area and
finally a bound file of Game Commission bulletins.

The state library came next and there, with
the help of the librarian in the reference room,
she compiled a list of books she could borrow for
a month at a time if she went to the lookout;
books on weather, timber problems, fire hazards
and fire fighting.

She found books written by lookouts, but King
had warned her conditions had changed greatly
since the war; much that was primitive had been
replaced by modern living equipment. Telephones, with the ever present problem of keeping lines cleared, had given way to two-way
radios; lookouts were insulated from electric
strikes, and of course many new towers had been
erected.

Reasoning that the basic job of a lookout was
still the same, Tess borrowed these books. She
wanted to know how other girls had occupied
the lonely hours.

Late that afternoon she called her former

office and found her successor was working out well. She learned she was supposed to be taking a much needed vacation and assumed Matt had used that to cover a period he would call, "time to come to your senses."

In the evening she called Matson and told him she would return Saturday for the weekend only.

Calling her housekeeper was a luxury Tess could not afford. The elderly lady, who had served her father for years, was completely charmed by Matt Speares. Anything she would say would be relayed on; the note she'd left would have to suffice, a note telling her she could now plan to retire on the annuity the judge had set up for her years before. Tess knew how welcome that would be; the big house had become a burden to both of them.

Tess spent the next day with pad and pencil working out the disposition of four generations of Palmer possessions, thinking fervently time after time, Thank goodness I wasn't a boy. I'd have felt I had to carry on.

Driving to her chosen district headquarters the next morning, Tess had a feeling of coming home, a sense of possessiveness and pride in the neat lawns with sprinklers whirling, and in the young firs around the park-like grounds.

Three days later Tess headed back for her home town, wondering if all she had heard had been imprinted upon her subconscious; if it would rise to the surface when and if it were needed.

The big house looked alien now. Reluctantly Tess entered and switched on lights, though the last of the afternoon glow lingered.

Even if I don't go to a lookout, she thought, I'm going to get out of here immediately.

She packed all of the next day except for the time spent with the auctioneer Matson had suggested she call it.

To one side went the few articles she would use at the lookout. A woolly Hopi rug, blankets, clothes and a few choice books. To minimize household cookery she had packed a toaster, an electric frying pan and a dutch oven before she realized there'd be no electricity.

When she went down to shop for groceries to carry her through the weekend she carried the list she'd made out and thought, Well, why not try it and see if I can camp in a lookout and have simple, balanced meals?

She would have fresh meat once a week when supplies came up unless there was a fire. She supposed dry ice would solve the problems, or a small ice chest, but why bother? Fresh vegetables would keep, wrapped in damp cloth or cellophane bags and immersed in water.

She'd talked to some of the older lookouts at Guard School and learned much about the food problem, the advisability of keeping staples on hand to carry her through in case of a major fire when all rolling equipment was busy with emergency transportation problems.

Tess made one foolish purchase; a bottle of imitation vanilla, because with it came a small copper-sheeted kerosene lamp which would hang on a wall. And while a lookout actually had no walls, she would find some way to hang it as a bedlamp for those nights when sleep refused to be wooed.

So engrossed was she in her delightful game of make-believe it was dark before she realized one part of her had been tensed against a visit from Matt.

Instead came a messenger boy with a letter.

For a long time Tess stared at it, dreading to open it lest he, with his lawyer's way of stating pertinent facts, might spoil her present happiness with doubts of the course she was taking. Then abruptly she opened it and read:

"Dear Tess,

I heard you were home, but as you didn't call me I assumed you weren't ready to see me.

I'm confident you know how unfairly you've treated me and can believe only that you are being influenced by some other man.

When you are ready to see me, let me know. As ever,

Yours, Matt."

She didn't sleep well. The windows were grey when the telephone rang. A strange hour, she thought, and then heard the long distance operator say, "Ready with your call, Mr. Winston."

"Miss Palmer, would it be possible for you to report here immediately? The girl on Phantom Peak was frightened out last night. The boys are bringing her down now."

CHAPTER 5

There was no one in the administration building when Tess reached it, but there was a typewritten list on the counter, and it drew her attention.

Typed on the paper were the lookout stations and their attendants. And at the bottom was Phantom Peak, with the name of Tess Palmer.

Tom Winston, coming in, smiled at the expression on her face.

"I wasn't nearly as proud when I had *cum laude* added to my honors," she told him.

Winston invited her in to wait for the truck that would take her up. The final few miles needed more power than her light car could offer.

"The girl who's coming down was frightened away, as I told you on the telephone. It seemed she heard many strange sounds. Last night she insisted some woman was being murdered. She'd heard her cry at half-hour intervals, and while I assured her no one being murdered could cry so many times, I couldn't convince her she was probably listening to a cougar.

"By the way, have you ever heard a cougar?"

"Yes, and I still jump out of my skin at that first unholy shriek. I used to go camping with my father. He insisted it was a love call, and I said if it were, I was through with love."

"More likely triumph over a good dinner. She also insisted someone was whispering. We told her that was the wind through the guy wires. Actually we had our doubts about her. She was a little too young and too accustomed to a large family. Yet her other qualifications were good enough for us to give her a try-out."

Tess listened soberly and admitted she anticipated being frightened. "But I've been fortunate. Dad always made me face the fright, and it's strange how it fades away when the cause is located, even if it is real."

"Such as?"

"Rattlesnakes."

"That's one thing you won't have to worry about. Not on this range. Too cold for them. By the way, what was your father's cure-all for the diamondbacks?"

"Stand still and, if you must, aim straight at the head and shoot to kill. I had to once. I'm glad it happened but hope it won't be necessary again."

They talked then of her duties as lookout. There would be the hourly check-up from central lookout. She'd heard the words, "Six-O-Forty check call," and would come in with her own call number, "Five-five-five." She must remember if she missed this check call it would mean someone would be called from other duties to investigate. It was her radio protection; assurance that no more than an hour or so could pass without help being sent to her.

Al King came in to take her up.

"I got you into this," Al said, as though he had to give a reason for his presence, "so I asked if I could see you settled. The warden will be up to check in a day or so. This hot stretch is unusual at this time of the year. We'll probably have electric storms, and while it isn't likely we'd have a major fire from a strike, fire wardens always prepare for the unlikely."

Tess blessed the weather; it was putting her where she wanted to be.

And she was glad Al was taking her up, though she didn't know why. She assumed it was because she felt she knew him better. If she must make a fool of herself with silly questions, she'd prefer asking him.

When they'd driven into the foothills, the shade and resinous perfume of young fir wove a lethargic spell over Tess and she leaned back.

"You look tired," Al remarked frankly.

"I am. I tried to close out four generations of living in one day. Professional packers and movers will take over where I left off. Actually I think it's let-down. I've been carrying the expense and burden of a huge house since Father died. Now the load's off my back, I realize how heavy it was."

"Meaning you don't believe in tradition?"

"Just the spiritual assets, intangibles like character and assurance, rather than pride in the achievements of ancestors," she said thoughtfully.

They were silent until they topped the last rise and Tess saw her new home rearing high above—a cabin in the sky, washed golden in the noon sunshine.

"Isn't it beautiful?" she asked.

Al pulled up in the leveled parking area and turned to her. "How do you feel about electric storms? I know you've nothing to fear, but will you think it beautiful when the lightning comes striking down as though it had you marked?"

"I'll remember what you told me, that I'm safer there than in the average house. Besides, I'll probably be too busy watching for strikes to have time to be afraid."

When bags and bundles had been carried just under the tower, Al commented on the small amount of things she'd brought and said it was good.

"Revolt," Tess told him. "I need a vacation from *things*."

When she started up to receive the loads from the windlass, he told her to take it slow until she was accustomed to the change in altitude, and she, with some two hundred steps ahead going straight up, was more than willing.

The cabin seemed changed now that the shutters were up, forming a shelter from sun and rain over the catwalk. It made the drop seem less precipitous, with less sky immediately overhead, the cabin less exposed.

For half an hour Tess swung cartons, bags and containers onto the catwalk; then Al joined her and carried the heavier pieces inside.

There was one box she didn't recognize, and Al admitted it was a lunch box the cook had put up for them because she wouldn't have had time to settle down by noon.

Unpacking books while she unpacked the box, he commented on the titles. "You're going to enjoy your stay up here. There'll be long, rainy days when you can't see beyond the edge of the catwalk."

"I'm going to enjoy this more." And from a small box Tess brought out a stout, round-faced clock with an illuminated dial. "I don't think I'll be too preoccupied to forget time, but with an alarm set I know I'm safe."

Al watched her, an amused smile crinkling around his grey eyes. With her he sat at the small table looking west over the mountains to a white line they knew was the Pacific. For a centerpiece they had the clock.

Then, when Tess's teeth were firmly imbedded in a sandwich, it came, first a raucous sound, then a voice.

"Six-oh-forty, check call."

The chair went over as Tess sprang up. At first she looked out as though she could see the high peak and the woman making the call; then she swung to the radio and stared at it accusingly.

"Five-five-five," she managed breathlessly.

And then she looked at Al in horror. "I haven't given a check look at my area once since I've been up here."

"I have," he chuckled, "or did you think my trips on the catwalk were to admire the mountains?"

He assured her that after she'd been there a short time she would become so conscious of her work it would become a part of her.

When they had finished lunch he took her down to scout the immediate area around the lookout tower. Beyond the level ground there was a sharp drop on all sides. Al warned against wandering around in a cloud and advised her to keep to the road

Threading a path through brush, he took her down to a spring. He didn't anticipate her ever having to go down for water, but if all equip ment happened to be busy here was an emer gency water supply.

They talked of wild animals on the way back. This area had deer cougar brown bear and wildcat, though she might not see any of them. There were a few coyote.

On the lookout again, he took her around, identifying permanent smokes. These were legitimate fires in mills. Burning permits in her area were canceled because of the present hot spell. She'd be told when any were issued, if they were, during heavy rains, so she could identify them. There'd be none when the normal dry sea son came on

Tess had been ready for her second check call and came outside thinking surely she must see the slender thread that wove a cobweb of com munication between mountain tops.

Now Al discussed the importance of becoming acquainted with her own area, studying it, and identifying it on the map. Fires would be re ported by degrees of latitude and longitude, bu knowledge of the terrain would give her the ease of familiarity

And he spoke of how contours could change with changing lights; how a mountain, like a headland, could stand out sharply at one time and, with the sun in a different position, merge with its background.

He also talked of the interdependence of look outs. Each tower had its blind spots; areas imme diately under the lookouts were hidden by hills or cliffs, but visible from a nearby lookout in another area.

"Report everything," he advised, 'that gives the dispatcher a cross-check or confirmation and when you're putting men into the field where there's thick timber and where the smoke is visi ble only from above, a shade of difference in degrees can mean time lost locating the danger spot."

"In other words we're the eyes," murmured Tess.

He indicated imaginary smokes at different spots and gave her practice locating them with the fire finder.

Carefully at first, as though it would hump up and hiss at her, Tess swung the alidade, sighted and read the azimuth. Then gradually her confidence increased. If she continued to practice she would be able to give a creditable performance when the warden came up.

Al left at mid-afternoon. Tess walked down to the truck with him and stood looking at him a moment.

"I have you so mixed up with this job,' she mused, and stopped.

"Then we'll have to see that you like the job," he returned and, starting the motor, swung down the mountain.

CHAPTER 6

When Tess awakened in the morning the sky was frosted gold Rested, she made an early breakfast, one eye on the world outside. So much world but so little of it distinct yet. The snow peaks to the east seemed like sails riding a night blue sea. Getting into a heavy coat, she went out to watch this sea break into ridges and valleys as the sun mounted the horizon

Tess thought of Matt. She should write She wondered ˙ Matson had told him where she was, how to reach her. And she hoped he hadn't Yet she did owe him an apology for running away so abruptly.

Maybe tomorrow she'd be ready to write O maybe later after she'd become a little bored with life alone on a mountain top. Or would she ever? She heard of lookouts who hibernated in the winter, existing until it was time to move back to their idea of living in their lookout tower. But they were older people who'd already had their fill of marriage and children

Sleep came later that night She was rested now. She'd even listened to a newscast on her small battery radio. There had been much talk of the weather. Heat records were broken and dry spell records for this time of the year were announced.

However, almost everyone, including one Tess Palmer, was enjoying it.

There were a few exceptions. One called on her the next morning, a man who literally carried one hundred and sixty thousand acres on his broad shoulders.

Tess had read that forest fire wardens were not a relaxed, happy lot. Their world was subject to so many unpredictable events: lightning from the sky and man from the earth, the lightning giving more warning of the holocaust. it could cause than man, who would try to hide it.

Not that Mr. Mondy looked unhappy as he came up into the cabin. He seemed pleased that she'd been available on such short notice. He was manning all of the towers he could at the time, but his schoolteacher lookouts couldn't come until school was out.

"According to our forecaster this heat wave will probably end in an electric storm, but the woods haven't dried out too much and there'll be rain with the storm. But," he added, "that doesn't mean we don't want every strike reported and every area watched."

Tess demonstrated her familiarity with the fire finder, and then they went outside and she made use of her map study of the last two days.

The warden couldn't stay for lunch; he was getting the summer fire suppression crews ready for action, visiting all parts of his district, checking with deputy district wardens, and giving the equipment still another once-over.

"Oh," he said at the last, "mail. I brought your mail up. Anything you want me to take down? Had you forgotten anything in groceries? Something tells me King will be up on his next rest period, but that won't be until after the storm."

There was quite a roll of mail. Tess fingered it absently; most of it had been sent on from her home. Now she was more interested in the storm.

"Has it announced its intentions?" she asked.

"Not exactly. Couple of lows in the Pacific; the usual one off the Aleutian Islands. Of course, both of them may blow north. Then again they may not. Be a few days, I imagine."

Tess noticed he checked the insulating wires before he left and felt comforted. She was as safe as she would be in a cave.

And then when the sound of his motor had died away she turned to the mail. Letters from girl friends she laid aside; circulars went with them. She'd look at these during twilight's lonely hour.

There was no letter from Matt. She couldn't picture Matt going to Matson for her address. And there was a letter from Matson.

Tess paused for a check look, then waited until her hourly check call was over.

She perched on the edge of a chair and opened the letter, read a line, then read the balance quickly.

"—injunction against the City purchasing your home."

Oh no, not after I've sold the furniture and moved and—

"—haven't been able to learn who's behind this move. However, the injunction was brought by a newcomer here, Carl Jennings. As soon as I can learn the motive, or rather, who's behind him, I'll advise you."

"You don't need to." Tess spoke aloud. "It's Matt. It's the only way he can save it for himself."

And then she thought of what the loss of this money would mean to her next winter.

More than anything she felt a deep resentment toward Matt for placing the millstone of the big house back around her neck.

An hour later Tess sank into the cabin's one easy chair, relaxed into it as though she were part of it.

This is crazy, she thought. For some reason I can't stay angry. I can't even hold onto a worry. Now why?

That morning in the courtroom when she'd been so disturbed, she'd thought she wanted a mountain top to think things out. Now she had, to her, the most beautiful mountain in the Coast Range. And she wasn't thinking. Not about her problems.

There's nothing I can do about anything down there, she thought, looking north toward her home town, so why fret about it? There isn't a single solitary thing I can do until the fire season's over. Why spoil three months thinking about something that may never happen?

She'd let those poor unfortunates who didn't have lookout towers quarrel over her possessions. She had all she needed for the present, and affectionately she looked around her small fourteen-by-fourteen domain.

I'll not even think about Matt, she decided, going back to her sky and horizons.

One thing she learned in her psychology class was the impossibility of keeping the mind blank for any length of time. Matt's image met her to the east, the south, the west and the north.

So one puts the opposite of the unwanted thought into the mind. Now who is the antithesis of Matt?

Al King seemed to spring into that vacant

place, and Tess, for what she called a purely therapeutic reason, began recalling everything she had learned about him. And Matt crept back in as contrast.

King hadn't Matt's height or his striking good looks; nor did he think any girl who looked at him would promptly fall on her face in adoration.

He hadn't Matt's dynamic personality either. Tess looked down on miles of mountains and thought Al King's strength was rather like those mountains. There was no nervous energy causing them to spring up with a "look at me" air. They simply were.

And looking at the mountains, Tess saw a small pencil line of smoke rise in the still air and rushed for the fire finder.

Maybe she was making a fool of herself, but she'd sooner be made a fool than miss a report.

"That can be on the Veerhausen ranch," the dispatcher told her, "but watch it. I'll send one of the boys up."

Half an hour later the smoke stopped so abruptly Tess realized it had assistance from the Tyee Fire District. The rancher had been clear ing a strip beyond his own fence line and wanted to get rid of the evidence.

He hadn't stopped to think of the days of dry weather they'd had. He hadn't thought there'd be enough of a fire to warrant him taking time from spring chores to go after a fire permit. Actually, he hadn't believed anyone would see it, tucked under a hill.

Tess went back to her thoughts. A northbound plane moved across the sky, closer to the range than usual, and Tess was delighted to see it at eye level, though its roar seemed to disturb her ears and her equilibrium.

She wondered if it had been Al King who'd gone out to check on the smoke and what course of action was being taken. A warning perhaps, for this would be civil action; trespass and supposed destruction of private property. The fire season hadn't been officially opened yet.

And of course the rancher had a point. A fire started in his neighbor's brush could consume his grain fields and buildings.

Moving to the west, Tess experienced a moment's surprise. Surely Mt. Wyeast hadn't skipped the Columbia and raced south to take

root in the Pacific But just off shore alone in
the western sky was a perfect cone The first
cloud she'd seen since she'd come to the tower

On her last round she found it had disinte
grated; was riding the sky in small golden balls
with flattened undersides

Tess barely touched her evening meal. Something more than a lowering barometer seemed to
be affecting her. Perhaps sleep was indicated,
but she had no desire for it and went back to the
catwalk.

Now the sky was burnt rose with smudges of
black a hot color and in the valley the purple
was indigo

She thought of the big home she had left and
in a frantic moment wondered if she'd acted on
impulse in trying to give it away She felt piqued
because Matt seemed to think more of the building than of her

Now nobody wanted the house A protective
urge swept over her She wanted to race down
the mountain, hurry back to the house and gather
it into protective arms.

It was as alone as she, and never had she had
such a devastating feeling of aloneness. Here she

was, suspended above an uncaring world, without a human being within miles, and above an equally uncaring sky veiling its stars.

The forest below was in an ugly mood this night. Sounds came up to her: a rush, a crackle of brush, a despairing scream of some small animal.

And then the wind rose, not the four o'clock sea breeze she'd known all of her life but something from the far west that turned whispering wires into wailing voices.

Darkness had come to the cabin. Cockleshell, she called it as she turned in. In trying to light the lamp her fingers fumbled and the fragile mantle was crushed.

The little copper-based lamp gave a sturdy blaze and Tess, looking at it, laughed. Imagine such a gleam coming with a bottle of imitation vanilla. And how happy she'd been the day she'd bought the combination; how eagerly she had looked forward to the then doubtful life in a lookout.

She turned to her books and found one written for laymen, and was soon chuckling over the ancient methods of forecast from Noah to

Aristotle. The ages between had added much in-formation, but she wondered how future gener-ations with their increased knowledge would look upon this era.

Oh, by that time they'll probably call the shots, she decided sleepily. Maybe then wars will start over who's to have rain in a given area; the farmer needing it for his crops, or the nearby city requiring sunshine for tourists. Today's meteorologists don't know what an easy time they're having.

When she awakened an unfamiliar air hung over the cabin. Sitting up, she saw an overcast sky, and when she went out found the valleys cut off from sight by a sea of low clouds.

Walking to the west, she saw movement im-mediately below. But it was merely a deer made brave by this comforting blanket of clouds.

With clouds at this level, other mountain tops stood out, isolated from the range proper. Tess could see other lookout towers; at least she knew that the particular deepening of color indicated them.

She wondered what problems the other women had carried up with them; if they could rid themselves of them as she had the previous day and if they came riding back on the night winds and were solved by the dawn.

She was reassured now. The injunction had been granted, but the city could still "show cause why the purchase of the late Judge Paulus Palmer's home, now the property of his heir Tess Palmer, should be made for the purpose indicated."

It was up to those bringing the injunction to prove the city at fault. And Tess didn't believe that could be done.

She had nothing upon which to base her belief that Matt had been fighting for time and used a cat's-paw to act in his stead.

But she knew Matt. Once he had a goal set firmly in mind, nothing must interfere in its ultimate achievement. By the same premise her pioneer ancestors could never have crossed the plains without pushing on regardless of conditions.

Clouds clearing from the valley were whipped on by a stiff breeze. To the west their replacements were rolling in, merging with a sky which had thickened steadily.

At noon, after the check call, Tess was surprised to hear the dispatcher's voice. "All set for a little excess electricity this afternoon?" he asked. "Doesn't look too bad. You're not nervous about your first storm up there?"

"Excited," Tess confessed, "but I always become excited in a storm. That's not unusual." And she promised that excitement had nothing to do with her morale. She'd be watching for any strikes.

The storm began shortly after five o'clock, the first roll of thunder coming in as a surprise.

Now Tess turned her attention to the southwest and was rewarded by her most intimate view of lightning. It was well out of her range and she watched with interest.

"Special sound effects," she murmured as it moved nearer, the vibration of the thunder rattling a cup and saucer she'd left on the table.

Satisfied, the storm moved on, circling the valley and heading for the Cascades. Tess watched, puzzled.

This wasn't like any lightning she'd ever seen before. It seemed to drop out of the sky like a silver wire that had been coiled tightly. "In knots," she whispered, and felt the affair anti-climactic.

Darkness came early and morning brought the sun, but the atmosphere hadn't been cleared by the storm. The heat had a steamy quality, and even at this height Tess felt uncomfortable.

Al King made a quick visit that afternoon. Matson had telephoned headquarters. He was sending a letter he'd like to reach Miss Palmer, if possible. The answer could be telephoned.

"Here, here," soothed King as Tess read, "don't get your back up. Nothing's worth that."

"Then tell me why men assume a woman has no brains at all?" she demanded. "The fact that I announced my decision to sell my home suddenly was no reason for even my attorney to consider it an impulse. My goodness, my father felt it was a burden for years. And so did I. And I don't care how many injunctions are brought against its purchase. If the city doesn't buy it, I'll sell the land to a supermarket. That'll stop them," she prophesied.

"Why do you want to sell?" he asked.

"Would you like a three story house plus base ment to heat and care for, if you were alone?

And would you like to pay taxes on such a place situated in the heart of a city? And what does one do with a ballroom these days?"

"Personally, no," he agreed. "But then I have no desire for the type of income it would take to maintain such a home."

"And if one hadn't that type of income and still had the house? Honestly, Al, it seemed that every time we wanted anything or wanted to do something, the house had to have a new roof, or new gutters, or the termites had come in."

He nodded but looked puzzled. "Then you've no fondness for the old place, no memories?"

"Of course I have," she cried in exasperation, "but I can have those memories without the burden of the house, can't I?"

He had headed down through the trap door before he threw up the reason for his comment. "Good. In forestry we usually try out several houses before we settle into one for any period of time."

He'd pulled the door down after him, and before Tess could awaken to what he'd meant he had reached the truck.

"Well, really," she whispered, then wondered

why she was so pleased, and raced out to call down, "I didn't tell you what to relay to Matson."

"But you did," he returned. "I'm to tell him your decision to sell the house was based on the same good common sense all lady lookouts show."

It could have been the sunset. Giant cumulus clouds in the west burned in gold, rose, amber and purple, and Tess had a box seat for the show. Possibly it just could have been Al King's visit. But something had chased away her loneliness.

With the sunset a cold wind sprang up and, going into the cabin, Tess lighted the small heater, her kerosene table lamp, and put on the coffee pot.

Imagine being cozy at this altitude, she mused.

Thinking of being cozy, she thought of the big house and how it had defied all efforts to give it the warm intimacy of a home. Unless the whole house was heated, unused rooms lurked like icy monsters ready to devour any warm air that leaked out through an opened door. She'd grown up to, "Tessie, shut that door."

Unbidden came the vision of homes provided

by the Department of Forestry. The one she'd seen up the river, green as the trees that flanked it and gay inside. A woman's whole life needn't be given to keeping it livable.

Unbidden, too, came the thought of Matt as a small boy in a small house, as her father had once seen him. Representing the suddenly widowed mother, Paulus Palmer had gone down to discuss wise handling of the money Mrs. Seares had received in the damage suit.

"Compact and neat as a pin," he'd reported to his young daughter.

As the next day progressed Tess felt she should give Matt more understanding. A steamy heat rose from the valley, and she found no pleasure or comfort even on the shady side of the tower.

A small house could be uncomfortable, she mused, and a big one desirable. But why can't he settle for something in between?

She thought of Al and his satisfaction with whatever living quarters were offered. But he worked with the forest. A residential address had no career value to him as it had to Matt.

Perhaps both were right according to where they stood. Visibility was erratic. Tess looked west and found a thin layer of mist obscuring her view. On the next round it rose out of canyons so much like smoke she wanted to race for the fire finder.

Sunset was not the hour of beauty of the previous night. The sky was dirty, smudged yellow and brown, with clouds boiling restlessly over the sea.

By mid-morning the next day Tess found her nervous excitement rising as rapidly as barometers were dropping. To the east the sky thickened, but to the west, clear in patches, towering cumulus clouds boiled up as though some genie were working in the heart of each.

I've never seen such thunderheads, she mused. If this wasn't Oregon I'd say the storm coming will be a dilly.

The coastal northwest rarely had electric storms of any intensity. Her father had remembered only two minor ones in his childhood. But of late they had been increasing in number and intensity.

Tess spent that humid day trying to ferret out the reason. In spare time she studied weather charts and books, but by murky mid-afternoon she wondered why she should be able to learn what professional meteorologists couldn't.

And why didn't she admit her only interest in these theories lay in her attempt to keep her mind off the storm? That her fear was mounting with the clouds that now swept in from the sea like Valkyries? Surely nothing else could make such weird sounds, battle cries.

The first volley of thunder caught her on the north side. She raced into the tower and tried to remember all she must do at the onslaught of a storm.

The second flash. No silver wire this, but a jagged bolt thrown from the sky. She made a note of it, though it was far south of her area.

Bolt after bolt was hurled through the sky, each nearer, until the seventh seemed to envelop her in sound as the tower vibrated and the stream of light shot downward past her fixed gaze.

CHAPTER 7

Had the tower been struck? Oh, surely it had. Tess closed her eyes, opened them and, looking, down saw a tree several hundred yards below still shuddering from the impact.

"Idiot!" she snapped, not referring to the tree.

Here she was with her first strike and hadn't sense enough to know it.

Fingers still trembling, she brought the alidade closer, made her findings and, as a second strike sounded miles east, made ready to send on the location.

Now how, she demanded of the world at large, can the dispatcher sit before that dangerous board in a storm like this and sound so calm?

Well, if he could, she could. She knew that five years ago a bolt had shattered a tree beside the district headquarters. The radio had been only a few yards away. It could have struck that as easily. Tom Winston wasn't in an insulated tower.

I might as well enjoy this, she decided, and began marking the progress of the storm, adding once, in proud confirmation, "It is a dilly, all right."

This time it didn't follow the mountains but walked the valley in long steps, each striking to the ground, each wreaking havoc on something or someone.

As the strikes moved on they heralded their path with a blue green light that turned silver and red gold.

Now she knew what Bev Robinson had meant when she'd said, "You're so interested in the storm you forget fear."

She had forgotten herself. She was merely a pair of eyes watching a stupendous cyclorama of action, and a mind intent upon any danger that might strike at the area under her care.

And then a cloud descended upon her peak

and veiled the scene, and only distant rumbling told her the storm was continuing on its way.

The second check call came, and she realized she had been watching for two hours; an hour and a half of active storm. She would learn there had been six strikes, besides the one she had recorded, within her fire district.

The rain which had flurried in at the heart of the storm settled now to a drizzle, and Tess, relieved of the steamy heat of the day, found she was hungry.

The evening news came through on her small battery radio as she dined on canned beef stew and packaged dumplings.

A trolley bus had been struck in Portland. Sixty-five people had escaped from the interior because the quick-thinking driver had thrown open the doors as the bolt, traveling along the trolley wire, had made contact. There were some injuries, none fatal, but the interior of the big vehicle had been gutted by fire.

Closer to her lookout were other casualties: two horses, one a five thousand dollar Arabian, had been killed as they took shelter under a tree. Numerous barns had burned. A mechanic, changing a tire, had had his arm paralyzed when a bolt ran its course nearby.

And there were numerous stories on the later news. A farmer had suffered an inexplicable burn from a nearby bolt, until the attending physician discovered the metal buckle on his belt matched the blister.

With each story Tess found her assurance increased. The storm had been, as she'd said, "a dilly," and she'd seen it through without panic. She had reported her strike accurately. The fire had been checked, put out immediately, as had all the others that started in the unusual storm.

The storm marked a change in Tess' attitude toward her position. It was as though she had been on trial, or was being examined and had received her diploma. Now she could settle down to routine.

For a week that routine was interspersed with electric storms. Small ones grumbled through the hills spitting fire occasionally. Days were uncomfortable, nights chilly, and then the heavy rains returned and threw a protective wet sheet over the forests.

Tess heard the first rumble of the supply

truck and was out expecting Al. But the boys who came told her he was off some place with the warden. However, she was delighted to see them, to talk without looking around, afraid of talking to herself aloud.

And they had much to talk about. Both were from State College, both were studying forestry. And although she'd graduated from there three years earlier, they had mutual friends among the faculty.

Of course they must stay for lunch; she could whip up biscuits in no time, and admitted modestly that she was a whiz with a can opener. Tess didn't mention the bottles of herbs she kept handy to add piquancy.

The boys left soon after a check call, and Tess went with them to the truck, then set off for a brisk walk.

Returning, she found herself lost in a cloud and was glad she'd stayed on the road. When the tower loomed through the mist she thought of it as, of all things, a harbor, and ran hastily up the steps, dropped the door and felt again a sense of security.

Time now for mail. There was nothing of

much importance; letters from friends who'd learned through Matson that she was maning a lookout.

Idly she read through the life of the previous summer which these girls were repeating this year.

And then her interest was pricked.

"We hardly see Matt any more. Someone said he was giving his all to some case; an appeal, they called it."

And—

"Why couldn't you have turned him back into circulation if you didn't want him?"

Another referred to the "row" she'd had with Matt. Word of their wedding plans had leaked out, then word of the cancellation, implying they'd quarreled.

For a moment she was furious; then she calmed down. With Matt such a matrimonial prize, it would never occur to the girls that she'd been the one to walk out on his plans.

She sat in the fog-encased cabin and viewed that episode dispassionately. Another girl would have handled it differently. She'd have been coy or emotional and somehow would have drawn Matt into some dramatic declaration of love.

"Oh, no, she wouldn't," Tess spoke aloud. "Matt's had dozens of girls of that type just waiting for the drop of a word. He's been very careful not to let them within danger distance."

By the time the next check-call came she had decided she had made the correct decision and would do it again. Until Matt saw her as something unrelated to the house, if he ever did, she intended to remain out of the danger zone herself.

She turned then to the town's newspaper. It gave her a peculiar feeling to see a photograph of her home on the front page, especially when she read the caption:

FAMOUS LANDMARK BONE
OF CONTENTION

This was the lead story, and it had been cleverly set with a column stating the city's viewpoint, a two-column box giving the history of the house, then another column stating reasons the city should not make the purchase.

Tess wondered if she was unable to read dispassionately, because she could not grasp the reasoning upon which the injunction was based. The citizen bringing the injunction was using the catch-phrase, "Build for a big future."

An excellent idea, but in a lumber town with business at a low ebb, houses empty, some business houses closed, the cost of a new building would lay a heavy burden on taxable property at a time the owners could least afford it.

Her home could be purchased at one fourth the cost of a new building, almost immediately house the books of the old city library which was condemned and, with minimum expense, provide space for other civic properties.

Something in the second story drew her attention back to it. Reading it the second time, she recognized the writer. There was no question in her mind now that Matt was behind the injunction. Every quoted phrase was his. He'd unquestionably written what his legal cat's-paw had given the press.

Aware the cloud had lifted, Tess went out to find a thick sky overhead, a valley below and hills around her; all the brilliant dark blue of Chinese porcelain.

A few lights came on as she watched, tiny pin pricks in the blue.

On the western side Tess found herself buffeted by a cloud wind from the southwest, the rain wind. Practically nothing could start a forest fire below this evening, and she went in to start the small heater.

She picked up the newspapers again, and on an inside page she found Matt's name. Matt Seares had asked for a continuance on the Decker Monrove appeal.

"But I thought he'd only made that appeal as part of the usual court ritual," she exclaimed, and cast her memory back to that morning in the court room.

After the verdict had been given Matt had approached the bench and asked for the right of appeal. His voice had been cool and, if she remembered correctly, parrot-like. She'd assumed he was merely doing what most criminal lawyers did: enter formal protest at the verdict.

"But he hasn't a chance," she said aloud, "unless," she mused a moment, "he's making a stand for probation. There can't be any new evidence. And Decker was convicted on direct evidence."

She puzzled over it all evening. It brought Matt back into focus more than his association with the injunction, where the house literally stood between them.

Matt, she knew, planned to run for District Attorney as soon as he felt he'd had enough courtroom experience.

Surely, she thought, he wouldn't go this far in a hopeless case to insure future votes from the loggers who'd been Decker's friends. He should know he'd be more likely to lose them. There was nothing complex in their thinking.

Well, she couldn't solve it from up here on the mountain, and what a blessing that was. She needn't be pressured into thinking about it too strenuously. Picking up a book on the early trails and roads of pioneers, she deliberately erased Matt from her mind.

Rain was sluicing down on the mountain the next morning. Tess, remembering her previous great need to be uninterrupted, to have time to lounge and read and above all to think, started pacing the cabin, wondering if this was the first indication of lookout fever.

A cloud parted to the northeast, and Tess saw a blue range appear for an instant. Barlow Pass? My, what a simple life those pioneers had. All they had to do was inch their way over mountains, cross chasms, and pray there would be food at the settlement to see them through the first winter.

Still feeling restless, Tess thought she'd risk a call to headquarters, ask if it would be all right if she went for a long walk. And then she had a vision of eager ears listening in from all over the coast range and she couldn't face it.

Imagine a veteran of the mountain peaks hearing her. Never! No, she'd wait until the next check-call, then go down to the spring and wash her hair. That would be sufficiently different to take her mind off herself. She might even rinse it as she walked home in the rain.

Pneumonia would settle all your troubles in one fell swoop, she answered herself.

It was fun. It was different. The woods smelled fresh and sweet and water dribbled down her neck every time she ducked under a fragrant bough. And returning was so much harder than going down, she was quite breathless when she reached the foot of the tower.

"With a haircut you'd look almost human," she informed her image and, after the mop was dry, tied it into a pony tail. Shetland variety, she decided and wondered why she hadn't asked other lookouts what they did about barbering.

If the skies cleared, Tess had six and a half hours before she could light the lamps and consider bedtime near. What would she do with those six and a half hours?

It was a perfect day for answering letters. She would write her girl friends all about the romance of being a lookout. Then, thinking of each girl, she wondered how she could present it so it would seem like romance to her. Each needed people in large numbers. Each needed amusement provided from an outside source.

As they had told her at headquarters, it took a rare combination of qualities to make a lookout. She'd thought she'd had them. She'd thought acceptance of one of the worst storms in the area had proven it. Actually, the real test had only begun, the most vital of all qualities had yet to be proven—her ability to remain at her post through endless, uneventful days.

Her boredom was shattered the next day. An overcast sky, like the inside of an aluminum kettle, was acting as a sounding board. She heard the four-geared truck on the first sharp rise and hurried in to put blueberry muffins in to bake, and the coffee pot ready to set on its burner.

Then she hurried back, afraid she would miss some of the sound, and gambled with herself about who would be inside the truck. The warden on an inspection trip? It wouldn't be supplies or water. Perhaps important mail? It would have to be very important for them to make an extra trip.

If it were, did she hope Al was bringing it? And why not? He belonged on mountain tops.

"Hi," she called as voices sounded below. "Coming up?"

"We are." It was Al's voice, but not as friendly as usual. Had she done something wrong? Had he been sent as an emissary?

"Straight on," he told whoever was with him.

Tess turned from slipping the final muffin onto a plate and for a moment had an intense desire to break into derisive laughter.

Matt Seares' head was even with the floor.

"Hello, Mohammed," she greeted him, and the laughter she'd suppressed gurgled uncontrollably in her voice.

"I'll admit," his shoulders appeared, "that your stubbornness is as immovable as a mountain." And then he was up on a level with her, the displeasure of the earlier moment replaced by his famous smile.

CHAPTER 8

Tess was conscious of Matt looking at her hair with disapproval even as his lips smiled. "Unless you brought a barber in your retinue, you'll have to like it," she said, and he was annoyed.

"Still trying to read my mind?"

"No, just your expression. Where's Al? Isn't he coming up? Al," she ran to call down to the khaki-clad figure striding away from the tower, "come back. Muffins hot out of the oven and coffee almost ready."

"Sorry; I have to take a look at that tree. It's pretty much of a snag, you know, and—"

"And you need some expert advice. Come up, and we'll all go down on an inspection tour."

"Tess," Matt was right behind her, "I told

King I wanted a little time to talk to you alone, or are you afraid to face me alone?"

"Afraid? Matthew lad, I am a lookout. We gals fear neither man, beast nor lightning, particularly lightning. Now, I know how a beast or a man will strike. Lightning, on the other hand, is unpredictable. Al, you are coming, aren't you?"

He came with reluctance and amusement. "Just for coffee and one muffin. We haven't much time. The Chief okayed the trip because Mr. Seares said something about official business."

"If it's official I need a witness. This man's an attorney representing the other side."

"Tess, you're misreading—"

"No Matt, I'm not. I've typed too many of your briefs not to know every pet phrase of yours. I don't know the man who brought the injunction against the city's purchase of my house, but I do know who wrote the article in the paper."

"All right, so I tried to save you from doing something you were going to regret later on. How are your sons going to feel when they learn you signed away their heritage in a fit of temper?"

"Well," Tess punched holes in a can of cream," if they're anything like their maternal grandfather, they're going to say, 'Good for you, Mom.' And stop making Al uncomfortable. We sound like a prelude to a divorce hearing."

"I didn't come up to quarrel," Matt informed her in his best courtroom manner.

"Good. Wash that down with a cup of coffee."

"I came," Matt went on doggedly, "to tell you the hearing is set for next Wednesday and to arrange a release for you so you could be present."

Tess leaned back against the table. "Matt, when are you going to quit quitting for me? I don't want a release. A lookout isn't something that can be replaced with a flick of the wrist. Besides, there is no reason for me to be present. This fight is between the man bringing the injunction and the city. I'm merely the innocent bystander."

She looked at Al King. "He didn't go to Mr. Mondy, did he?"

"Couldn't. He's down at Bexar. We caught

him by short-wave."

"Good. Now listen. Except for sickness or accident, or of course being fired for inattention to duty, I am not going down off this mountain until the fire season is over."

"And you intend to go on with the sale of the house?"

"If the city won't take it, a supermarket will. Of course, they might pay more. On the other hand, they might not; they'd only want the land."

Matt absorbed this and a muffin with equal displeasure, then, drawing a deep breath, began, "Tess, Mrs. Matson told Adele that you thought I cared more—" He stopped and glared at Al.

"Don't look at me, fellow," Al told him. "In my outfit we're sworn to uphold and protect the forest. This gal's so much a part of that protection I don't dare leave until she gives the word."

"That's worse than a judge snapping, 'Motion denied,' isn't it, Matt?" soothed Tess. "Because you lawyers always manage to slip in your say-so before the jury is told to disregard it." She thought a minute. "Well, maybe after Al has worked his way through some more muffins we'll let him look at his tree. It's within shouting distance."

"No more muffins," he stated sternly.

"How am I going to eat my way through the eighteen left?"

"I could come back," Al's voice was serious but his eyes were dancing, "another time," he added, and Matt turned to look at him really for the first time.

Tess understood why and didn't blame Matt too much. For three years, practically ever since she'd left college, she had gone out with no one else. She'd given him every right to assume there could be no other man in her life.

Now, she reasoned, he was questioning this. Until this moment he had looked upon Al King as no more than a chauffeur who would take him to his destination. He would be courteous, would remember Al's name forever, but it would never have occurred to him to look at this fellow in work-stained khakis as a rival.

Al slipped quietly away, and when he reached the ground began whistling a popular march, his way of assuring them he was out of earshot.

Tess listened, smiling. And suddenly Matt

barked, "You've changed. Oh, more than that hair style. You're—"

"No longer a case of arrested development?" she asked. "It's not your fault I moved around in a fog so long. Not altogether. Of course you've had more experience than the average in using persuasive arguments. It's your business to sway juries.

"I was brought up on court fare. It wasn't until I saw a court literally condone grand theft that I woke up and begin to question."

"I could explain that, Tess."

"That's what I was afraid of, Matt. Explanations, glossing of facts and swaying juries with emotionalism."

"The Decker Monrove jury wasn't swayed," he countered bitterly.

"It wouldn't have helped if it had been. The judge canceled any leniency when he gave it his directions."

"Then you think Monrove should have been freed, or given probation?"

Tess sighed. "Oh, Matt, no. But look at it from another viewpoint. Within a few hours a man guilty of theft with firearms is given a long sentence for stealing less than fifty dollars. A man guilty of theft by corruption, the theft of thousands in public funds, is given probation."

Matt smiled reluctantly. "Spoken like a Palmer, Tess. One reason I came up was to talk about Decker. I had the hearing on his appeal set to work up fresh evidence."

"For me, Matt?"

"For you, Tess."

"Wrong answer," she returned, and went out for a swing around the cabin. The clouds had lifted and a watery sun shone through.

Matt followed her, and they stood for a moment listening to the ringing sound of an axe, then a crash.

"The Forest Service protecting the good timber from the bad," Tess commented, and walked on.

Matt asked about Al King. Was it his business to weed out timber? Wasn't this privately owned land? Why, if he held any position at all, should he do a flunky's work?

"I believe," she said thoughtfully, "it's because all of them are more interested in the department as a whole than in their relation to it.

If they chance upon a job that needs doing, they don't stop to worry about protocol, or losing face. They think of a danger in relation to the whole."

Matt's quick mind grasped that and used it to his own advantage. "Then if they saw their department buying a building that would cost more to put into use than a new one, they'd try to stop it and reconsider."

"The house again," sighed Tess, and went back to the cabin.

He said they had so little time to be alone and he had so much to say, especially about the wedding plans. He supposed he should have consulted her first, but as she had no family his thought had been to relieve her of all the fuss and expense.

Al returned whistling but they didn't hear him. When he topped the first flight he couldn't help hearing every word Tess spoke; her voice expressed exasperation and something else he couldn't define.

"No, Matt, no. It wasn't that. Don't you realize you've never once asked me if I would marry you? You've never brought love into the picture.

You've treated me as some especially valuable piece of furniture to be stored with a friend while my setting was being redecorated.

"Marriage on such a basis would mean that I, as a piece of furniture, would be carried back in, set into a spot you'd chosen and left there to be pointed to with pride.

"I seriously doubt if you've ever seen me apart from the Palmer house. You've made that such a goal in your career—"

"Oh, forget the Palmer house," roared Matt, and nearly knocked Al off the stairway as he plunged down.

King beat a hasty retreat and looked up.

"Hey, Redhead, want anything special on the next trip any of us make up? I'll be going into town this week."

"You might bring me one of those little barber kits." Tess's voice was clear and still angry. Then she added, "No, by darn, I'm going to let 'er grow."

"It's your head," Al returned philosophically.

"It's my hair," she retorted, and he shrugged. Somewhere he'd heard one should always let a woman have the last word. Besides, he was relieved she wasn't weeping. That meant something. He wasn't exactly sure what, but something.

Of one thing Al was sure. He wouldn't have to create conversation on the trip down as he had on the trip up. This Matt Seares wasn't going to be in a talking mood.

Tess stormed around the cabin until the next check-call, then sought the ground and stormed around the tower and down the road and back. One handicap in a fourteen by fourteen was one's inability to walk off anger without danger to the anatomy.

She felt much better by evening, better than she had since she'd come to Phantom Peak. She'd felt she had left important business unfinished at home. Now she'd taken care of that. Now Matt knew exactly how she felt.

And wasn't Al King a joy to have around? She wondered how he would have reacted to the straight-from-the-shoulder talk she'd given Matt.

It's barely possible, she reasoned, that he'd never have put himself into a position where it was needed.

Twilight came, and the sky, which had briefly

cleared of clouds, began pulling its rain cap back on, a thin, slate grey cap.

"Shower cap," muttered Tess. Oh well, the Rose Festival would be over by the end of the week, and then the sun would come out. For some reason the officials could never out-guess the weather. She remembered the time she'd been queen of a float and had started out sitting in a mammoth fluff of green, and had ended sitting in a puddle of water looking more like a dryad than a queen.

Other peaks were wearing night caps of mist, dreary grey white, and she turned to the part of the valley that was visible. A few lights were very far away.

Matt, in his way, had wanted to provide her with a lighted home, with the warmth of security.

And I'd have sat looking at the lamps while he was out exchanging brains at some important dinner.

Well, she'd have a light of her own and not be worrying about when a husband came home.

Warily she approached the Alladin light. Some day she'd conquer this monster. The beautiful moonlight glow it gave was worth sacrifice to her nerves.

"Got it!" she caroled in triumph.

Rain beat down on the tower, and she lit the small heater, pulled up the easy chair and picked up the book she'd been saving for just such an evening. It contained many chapters, each written by a different forester.

She was intensely interested yet, she felt Matt stood just outside the circle of light, demanding more thought. Lookouts could be a handicap at times like this. Below she could have sought friends, a theater, dancing, that would tire her to the point of exhaustion.

"Well, you wanted to come up here so you could think, didn't you?" she rasped, and could have sworn the rain stopped in mid-air and looked in to learn if she was going to answer her question.

She tried and learned something interesting. When she sat down to think a problem through, suddenly there wasn't any problem. At least none that mulling over would help.

True to her prediction, the sun came out the last day of the festival and promptly set about making up for lost time, breaking heat records all along the coast and finally bringing out the extreme fire hazard warning.

By the time the heat had made her feel ready to be served at a barbecue, a giant cloud pyramided up from the sea and gave her a busy evening trying to figure out what it was shaped like.

Other clouds entered the game, quarreled a little and, after dark, spat a bit of fire at each other. Then a cold breeze calmed them down and they spread a grey flank of sun protection over the strawberry and cherry pickers who, Tess knew from the radio, were toiling in the fields and on hillsides.

She thought of these pickers of the cool weather harvests, a good majority of them students earning money for clothes for the next year. She, up here, was actually related to them in occupation.

Had there been no Department of Forestry, no protection of moisture gathering, soil holding trees, there would soon be no rich, moist valleys for strawberries, no deep soil hills for cherry trees.

If there were no lookouts, fire could rage out of control before it was sighted and suppression crews brought in. While lookouts were at the bottom of the scale, they were an integral part of the whole.

And Matt had expected her to walk out blithely.

She wondered how the hearing had come out. Al hadn't brought up the supplies. She wasn't too sorry. A stretch of time between his involvement with her quarrel with Matt and his return would provide a comforting buffer.

June was nearing an end. Vacationers were beginning to stream out from the towns. Some would, she knew, find their way into the valley below the north bluff, and since it was neither federal nor state property, they would trespass in their desire for the very shade trees they might so carelessly destroy.

She guarded the area like a mother hen whose chickens had run wild and out of sight.

Al came early the next morning. The fire danger degree had been forecast and, though it was registered at minimum, he wanted to be back in case the humidity went into a fit of temperament.

"Thought this mail might be important," he remarked, handing a roll of it wrapped in newspaper. "Didn't stop for coffee. No, go on and read it. I'll brew my own."

It seemed natural that he should. She told him to use some eggs. It had been too hot to bake, and one thing she didn't need in the lookout was a brood of baby chicks.

Al went about his chore, one eye on Tess. And when her hands fell into her lap, still holding a letter, he waited.

"Matt withdrew the injunction," she said, then added, "Funny, isn't it? You can start something but you can't always stop it. A group trying to get into City Hall this next election promptly filed another. He'd given them the idea when he filed. Now they're making a project of it."

"And the supermarket?" Deftly he flipped the pan and the egg.

"That was a threat. It's one thing to turn it over for a library and museum. It's another to stand by and see your home razed for a business that will hurt the friends you've grown up with."

He made an egg sandwich, stood sipping a cup of coffee and watched Tess go out on the catwalk. Automatically his gaze followed her.

Even as he heard her cry he saw it, the thin blue spiral of smoke rising straight up in the still morning air.

CHAPTER 9

As Tess took the finding, Al was on the radio. The smoke was in another district. "Just reported," Tess heard the dispatcher say while Al waited for his orders. He'd have to go to the valley floor before he could head for the area. The warden would reach there first, but he might as well be on hand.

"Two to one it's those fellows who've been robbing the fish traps on the west side. A road crosses over in that area. Steven's been after them. Neat if we could bottle them up."

"Expensive fish fry," murmured Tess, still watching the smoke.

He gave her one last thought. "Don't worry about the house; we'll use it for retiring fire wardens. Going up three stories is like climbing mountains—"

Tess heard the quick uptake of the motor, then concentrated on the southwest. The smoke was flattening out as it reached the level of a high cut. That the problem with fires; the first thing they destroyed was visibility, usually of the lookout closest to the scene.

Remembering this was not her fire, she went around searching out other areas, realizing now how quickly what could be clear one moment could show smoke another.

Back at the southwest, Tess looked at the long range that cut at an angle toward the coast. The sides which had been Dutch blue half an hour earlier were now hazy.

Fish fry, she thought.

Al had told her of the fish traps downstream. Trout heading upstream were picked up by the traps, loaded into giant tank trucks and carried swiftly to lakes that had been cleared of their enemies, the carp, and were left to stock a new home.

There was a small percentage of pseudo-sportsmen who objected to the practice, for though they had a long open season they took the short view and would fish the stream bare if given their way. In time there would be no fish for them or anyone else.

Tess was still thinking of these men when she stopped for a quick lunch. The fire had driven away all her concern about the Palmer house. Now it returned, and she opened a newspaper to see if it contained any news of the new injunction.

The first page of her home town paper carried a complete story, but her eyes went to a caption which read:

"DECKER MONROVE'S
   APPEAL DENIED."

When she returned to pacing the catwalk, her thoughts dwelt on Decker and somehow involved him with the men who might have caused the fire, now no more than a faint grey pall. She supposed they might be classified together as men who took the law into their own hands.

Yet Decker seemed closer to her. His case was more personal, and as she walked around, eyes alert to any change within her basin of mountains, she thought of him as she'd known him through the years.

He'd been an appealing small boy, with large dark eyes and a sensitive awareness of his shabby clothes. Later defiance had replaced the shy appeal and Judge Palmer had said it probably stemmed from his mother spending money at the town bars. Decker would stand no criticism of his mother and had been known to strike a visiting County Relief agent in her defense.

She thought next of Decker's wife. Mona's family had drifted north with other migrant field laborers, found a place to settle, and Mona had entered high school.

But Mona wanted no roots; a childhood of following the crops had instilled a gypsy spirit. Tess supposed it was natural the handsome sullen Decker and the shrewd pretty Mona should gravitate toward each other. They were married in their senior year and left school before graduation.

Tess had seen Mona at the trial. Matt had brought her in, baby in arms, two others at her side. She'd grown slovenly, but the shrewdness was still there. And Tess wasn't blaming her for the change.

Evening came. She knew the fish fry fire was out, but the smoke still hung like a curtain before the higher range, and for the first time she felt completely alone on top of the world.

It was an awesome feeling, rather like Kipling's Mr. Tomlinson suspended between sky and earth and belonging to neither. Eagerly she went into the shelter of the cabin.

Time now to read and digest the mail. Letters were tucked into a magazine. Tess found one from Matt and sank into the easy chair, holding it, wondering what it would contain.

When she was through she went back to the catwalk to pace around more disturbed now than she had ever been. Matt's letter had been surprisingly tender. He'd said he could understand how much the change from an empty big house to a compact cabin could mean to her. He told her he had brought heavy influence on the man who'd brought the injunction against the sale of her home and he'd withdrawn. He'd been shocked when the reactionary group had filed. And then he spoke of Decker Monrove.

"I worked on that appeal, Tess, because I believed if you had faith in him he was worth fighting for. But after that cryptic, 'Wrong answer' I lost heart. Decker leaves for the penitentiary tomorrow. He's in a bad mood. I have an idea he'll spent most of his time in solitary."

He said more, and now Tess was faced with something new. Matt intimated that she, her quick words, were responsible for his having let Decker down; that Decker's final fight for freedom had been handicapped.

Am I to blame because Matt misread my words? Any fight for Decker should have been based on facts, not on the sentiment of anyone who'd known him in high school.

She stood staring angrily in the direction of her home town, then wheeled and looked at the first reflection of lights from the capitol. Decker was there, out on the eastern edge of town in one of the cream-colored buildings set back and surrounded by beautiful lawns he couldn't enjoy.

Juxton, Matt had written, had a good job, and arrangements had been made with his employer to set aside fifty percent of his wages to be returned to the funds he'd robbed.

She hadn't been able to make Matt understand how she felt about these two cases because she wasn't sure exactly how she felt. Or rather, she wasn't able to put her thoughts into words.

Life fell into routine. Around and below the scene changed. Stretches between timber that had been green turned tan, then grey. Down in the valley, the grain fields were like so many colored postage stamps.

On days when a sea wind had cleared the air, she could look across to the Cascades and often could see the blue of fire. Closer, there were grass and brush fires, smoke billowing up like storm clouds.

No fire permits were being issued, and cooking fires were allowed only in state and national parks where pits or stoves controlled the blaze and Park Rangers were around to watch. But there was always the element who believed in laws but believed they applied to the other fellow. After all, what was one little old picnic fire? They'd done it before and gotten by.

Gotten by. Tess carried these words on her walks around the cabin. People were strange. They made laws for their own protection, then felt they were putting something over when they violated them.

She saw the white blaze of head lamps enter the valley from the east. The fire department. Then behind, an ever increasing row of pin prick lights, cars that followed, onlookers jamming up the traffic lanes, standing around under foot, telling how the fire should be fought but keeping well away from any participation.

In another direction faint moving light lines showed her where farmers were using the dry night to work in their fields.

The final check call came, and Tess went to bed wondering about another law, a traffic law demanding vehicles pull to the side of the road at the sound of a siren. How many obeyed, and how many firemen lost their lives because someone thought it smart to outrace them?

Al came up late the next evening. The district had been lucky thus far, but the fire season tension was everywhere. All mobile equipment stood by unless on active duty.

"Now take this truck." Tess had walked down to greet him and watched him pat a fender. "I get in, say, 'Home, James,' and you'd never believe it, but he turns his nose smack up at Phantom Peak. Naturally I have to come along."

"Naturally," agreed Tess, and when she thought she wasn't watched added her pat to the fender.

They carried her few supplies to the lookout, then sat chatting, lookout fashion.

"One way for a gal to pick up a roving eye," Al commented.

He gave her a brush-up on conditions. The woods were closed down, which meant to the layman no more logging operations were going on. In short, no risks were taken of any spark jumping from a motor or blade. Loggers and lumbermen who had been educated the hard way over the past thirty years found a protection for themselves in the law of the department.

Deer hunting season would open in a couple of weeks. And then look out. Seasoned hunters were safe to be "let loose in the woods."

"But there is always that minority." Tess added to the accumulation of thoughts she'd had on Phantom Peak.

Al asked if she'd made any plans for the winter, and she shook her head. "Not yet. And I doubt that there'll be any action on the house until after the election." And then she smiled. "The queerest thing, up here it doesn't seem the least bit important."

Talking of it made her realize she had only a few more weeks on the tower she had come to look upon as an emotional haven. She knew, for one thing, she would have to settle the question of Matt when she went down, and she'd come to no decision about him yet. His letters, she felt, were even more convincing than his summations to the jury.

But she was no jury.

Al said he could keep his eyes open; sometimes there were good stenographic jobs open in

Forestville. He'd like to keep her in the district a little longer, although he didn't say why.

They sat in companionable silence after the last check call. Then he said he'd better be getting down the hill. But before he left he asked one final question, a question he'd apparently studied over for some time.

"Tess, are you getting what you expected out of this job?"

And she waited before she replied, "More, much more. I've felt useful, for one thing, though I've done nothing yet. And I've had time to sort out a lot of things in my mind and air them. And with the books you've sent up from the State Library, I've learned something tremendously important.

"Mr. Mondy once told me he looked upon his work as a 'job to do.' The usual understatement of the out-of-doors man.

"When I read and then realize that what is now desert or waste land was once forested, I began to understand that forest conservation is just about the most important job in the world.

"We hear a lot about statesmen and big industrialists and financiers, but to me the unsung hero is the fellow running around in a soot-stained, sweat-stained shirt trying to save the forests, the land and the water for these statesmen, industrialists and financiers to be big about."

"That's my girl," cheered Al. "If I wasn't caught in this blasted trap door, I'd plant a kiss on your intelligent brow."

"If you didn't have such a good cook down at headquarters, you could get through those trap doors easier."

He'd reached the ground when he thought of something and called up, "Did I tell you about your friend Decker? He got in a row at the pen and got hurt. He's in the prison infirmary."

"So soon," she said softly, but she knew that was the pattern he'd set long ago.

Nights were longer now in late August. Wakening, Tess scanned her horizon quickly and then stood a moment.

At first she had thought of her lookout as part of a cobweb, fastened by invisible lines to the tower on Central Lookout Mt. Then she became related to lookouts all over the state, then down the long line of mountains stretching from

Canada to the Gulf of California.

The heat was intense this Saturday morning. The valley looked baked, and she turned eagerly to the hills, pin-cushioned with campers. One couldn't blame people for wanting to get away from the heat, for seeking the still, cool green of the forest.

Winston called her shortly before twilight. They'd had a report of campers going into the forbidden territory below the north bluff. The state police were checking, but people who ignored signs, cut the wires of a fence and slashed young trees to make way for their car were capable of anything. It would be a good area to watch

And Tess watched until long after dark, though the report came in that the campers had evidently not found what they wanted and had driven out before the police went in. They'd found the spot they'd cleared for their camp. No fire had been built. They'd also made a careful survey there to be sure there was no other fire danger.

Tess offered, "I'll set my alarm and call you at intervals."

Reason told him it wasn't necessary. He'd had cross-checks from two other stations. But that uncanny sixth sense kept prodding. Yet, aside from a blaze, what could any of them see on this moonless night?

"I have an awfully good smeller," Tess offered.

"Okay, two o'clock."

Tess wakened groggily at two. There was nothing to see but the black velvet of night, punctuated by distant stars, and nothing to smell but a rich mixture of dying vegetation, the resin of conifers and a slight salty tinge from the distant sea.

There was no wind at dawn. Tess made a careful check, particularly to the north northwest, and kept her attention more or less focused on it as she made coffee.

She carried her cup out with her and stood on the catwalk staring, then raced in.

"Maybe I'm crazy," she reported. "I don't see smoke, but I could swear I see radiation rising above that rock." And she gave the location.

"Watch it!" Winston's voice was as calm as usual, but Tess had a feeling his mind was going into action.

Ten minutes later she saw curling fronds of grey, almost mist-like, on the edge of the bluff.

"You've got yourself a fire," Winston responded to this report. "You know what to watch for."

CHAPTER 10

The radio squawked. The second lookout across the canyon and eight miles to the north-west was getting a run-down on the path, now that it had lifted above the ridge previously cutting her view.

The warden came in on his radio from the point they'd chosen.

The dispatcher glanced out. The crew, having gulped breakfast, waited before the big building to the north, ready to ride. They'd had a few small fires this year. This one promised to give them a chance to show what they really could do.

Sunday morning, a few cars heading for early mass veered as a siren blared. An out of state car, lost on a back road, pulled over as a second siren sliced the hot still air, the truck catapulting past in the opposite direction.

Time now to evaluate potential help, to have it standing by if necessary. The lumber companies had fire crews. Sunday morning was the worst possible time to expect them to be on hand.

Phantom came in again. Smoke now enveloped her tower. Tess could see nothing to the north or northeast.

Even as he deployed crews, the dispatcher mentally worked back to the cause.

Last night, that car of campers was reported five miles downstream. The strip between the cliff base and the stream was no more than a quarter-mile wide at the entrance and dwindled to a small triangle that stopped abruptly at the slide.

Someone had once thought of making a summer home there, but boulders had a way of slipping loose and rattling down. Returning one spring to find the roof of the cabin caved in, they'd given up.

Yesterday's campers had not been of the usual type, the dispatcher reasoned. They'd deposited one member, probabaly with sleeping bag and back pack, some amateur mountaineer who'd taken a dare and vowed to scale that particular cliff.

The car had driven off and the man, obviously young or he'd have had too much sense to attempt it, had started off before the police came. Or else, seeing them, he had remained well hidden.

He'd used the last daylight hours to start his climb, found darkness overtaking him and, finding a wide spot, or one of the small caves made by erosion, had stopped for the night.

He needed coffee in the morning. He probably awakened to find the sky lightening a little. There'd be enough brush twigs around to start the little fire he needed.

He'd have reasoned there was no fire danger against a rock wall. The fact he'd been able to gather together enough dry twigs to start a fire wouldn't penetrate his reasoning.

He'd probably scuffed it out and started up as soon as he could see to put one foot before the other.

Then what? The overhang.

The dispatcher had a topographical map in

his mind. A man made panicky at having to re-
trace his steps could fall. Which way he went
down would depend upon the man; crouching,
inching along, or a misstep and over the side.
But he'd have passed the fire before it was under
way.

The sirens had barely faded when he put in
his call to the state police.

Tess had a half-hour of smoke. Then it leaned
toward the east and she could follow the se-
quence. The dry brush on the rock side had
burned out; the sea breeze coming in was heading the fire over toward the second growth on
that first hill to the east. They'd logged there this
summer.

And they wouldn't have had time to clean up
the slashings, she thought.

She heard the siren coming up the hill,
blocked out on turns, rising sharply along canyon
roads. And then it struck an even note and died
away and there was just the sound of the motors,
pulling.

"That access road cuts off to the right before
the last gate," she whispered.

Now she could really appreciate access roads.

Fire breaks, yes, but more than that, time saved in reaching the fighting line; means of taking tank trucks within working distance.

A veer to the south and Tess reported it.

The wind was freshening. "So is the fire," she muttered.

It was out of her range now. The south lookout could see the side of the mountain directly under her hill.

I never thought I'd pray for a thunder shower, she mused. And after a minute, please disregard that prayer. With the woods this dry and all hands on deck here on Phantom, we can do without strikes elsewhere.

Obligingly the clouds flattened out to a white haze.

It was maddening to be up here above a cauldron and know nothing of what was going on, what was being accomplished, what odds were being fought.

And she couldn't call down for anything but pertinent information. That central radio was the heartbeat of fire suppression. Calls would be coming in from other lookouts, from the warden, perhaps from crews who called from other areas.

Not having too much experience, she could not picture how this fire had started; and not knowing the topography of that drop beyond the north side of the clearing, she could not understand how any blaze could have found enough fodder to creep across the rock until it found dry wood worthy of its destructive force.

Once she heard a peculiar sound and believed it was a signal that someone was hurt. Instantly her thoughts flew to Al, and instantly she was ashamed. She knew most of the boys now. They'd come up with water and supplies.

She understood now why the warden was rarely in his office. If a man had to know every nook and cranny within one hundred and sixteen thousand acres, all subject to fire at some period, that knowledge had to be an intimate personal thing.

By mid-afternoon she had decided to add to her list of a lookout's attributes, ability to keep frustration from sending one into a tail spin.

She'd reached that when the dispatcher called. "Stopped for lunch yet?"

Tess shook her head, then flipped the switch. "I even forgot breakfast. Just coffee."

"We have her under control now. That extra time you gave us this morning helped a lot."

"And just who kept me keened to the danger?" she asked.

A soft chuckle; then, "Time for your check call."

Tess found she was hungrier than she'd been in weeks, but she didn't want to take time to prepare anything. She'd been too keyed up to let down quickly.

The color of the smoke had changed; the roiling white and tan with streaks of black was thinning to transparent blue.

Just why, Tess wondered, do men always refer to everything from ships to forest fires as 'she'?

She made a sandwich and brought it out, munching as she moved around. The wind was dying, and the stench of the fire came sharply to the tower. People spoke lightly of wood smoke, as though it had but one odor. It had many, and the peculiar medley of smells in a forest fire didn't remind one of any cozy hearth fire.

Tess tuned in to the six o'clock news and, because she was listening for news of the fire, didn't catch the first part of the story, or the name of a man involved. The state police had found a fellow stranded on a tree, outthrust from North Face, where he'd fallen after attempting to climb to the top on a dare. His injuries were not serious.

He was being held, though, for questioning about a fire which broke out in the Tyee District near the vicinity in which he was found.

Tess straightened in indignation. And here she'd thought her fire would be the big news of the day.

She was ready for sleep long before dark. Below, she knew the mop-up crews were finishing off the last of the fire and that guards would be posted.

Except for the pale blue of the coast hills, ghost-like against the burnt orange of the sky, there was nothing to show there had been danger. It also indicated Phantom hadn't been the only area to have had a fire that hot day.

Nearby, the mountains were olive green, and Tess was again aware of the importance of lookouts. They could so easily have been black on such an evening. Fires had an unhappy faculty of sneaking through the brush and bursting into sight only when they were well under way. Only the overhead eye could watch the grey smoke in its first sly action.

Labor Day weekend was the next period of tension. Again man was loose in the woods. Tess saw black pillars of smoke, white-topped, mushroom up in wooded areas of the valley; rural fires.

But with the season drawing to a close she had other problems, personal problems.

The rains could start any time now, the lookouts be closed, shuttered for the winter. And what of the lady lookout of Phantom Peak?

She still had the big house. She still had enough furniture in storage to furnish the few rooms she had been using before she left. But the idea of going back was, in effect, like settling under a grey, monotonous sky. It was completely depressing.

An apartment. But where? Al had said he was going to keep an eye open for stenographic jobs in the district; that he'd like to keep her there awhile. And how long, if she read his meaning right, did she want to remain?

And if she didn't, what of the rest of her life?

She began to wish now that she had trained for some definite profession.

The first fall rain came, and Tess stood in it and held out her arms to catch the feel of the gentle drizzle.

Al came up in the midst of it and warned her not to let this fool her. "It does a lot of people," he said. "They think because it's rained all fire danger is over. It isn't. This first one barely dampens the crust of the duff. A few days of dry weather, breeze and sunshine, and the kindling is ready for the match."

Tess asked how much longer he thought the lookout would remain open.

"Depends upon the weather. The shoolteachers left this week, so the others will stay on until we have a soaker."

And then he asked what she was thinking about.

"Seasons," she replied. "Queer how you can feel them even when you're too high above the world to see the changes in gardens and fruit trees."

"The vine maple will be changing color soon," he told her. "Then you'll see patches of scarlet that look like flame. First ones may have you guessing."

He stayed for lunch, and Tess, sitting across the small table from him, aware of rain dripping off the shutter-roof, the warmth of the small stove, was vividly conscious of the companionable company.

When they were through he spoke rather abruptly. "You don't have to get high on a hill to think, Tess. I've been down under or out in the woods all summer, and I've been doing a lot. Maybe too much for my peace of mind."

"Meaning?" she asked.

"There are only x number of administrative jobs. Right now all are filled by fine, competent men. Those of us coming up have to wait for new districts or replacements. I don't want to wait. Besides, now I have something else I want to do.

"Talking to you, trying to sell you on the importance of forests, I sold myself. I'd say you were above the average intelligence, but you knew very little about the subject when we first met. Right?"

"Right," she agreed.

"And then," he smiled ruefully, "I found out how little I knew. I have a little money. I'd like to use it to travel to all countries interested in forestry. I'd like to study their methods of reforestation and of fire control and suppression. Oh, everything from the top administrator to—"

"The lowliest lookout?" teased Tess.

"Could be. Would you believe it's only recently some countries have used either the telephone or radio for an alert? They depended upon native runners or a man on a horse. Well, what do you think of the idea?"

"That it's completely fascinating," Tess replied honestly.

"Good." Abrupt as usual, he started to leave. "Think it over."

And he was gone.

Mail and a few supplies came in with a roar the following noon; the boys were in working blues with no time for small talk. They were heading back to college as soon as the forecasted storm struck.

Tess watched them leave and felt deprived of more than company. They knew where they were going; she didn't. There was Al and his talk of foreign forests, and Matt and his talk of going into politics, and it seemed to Tess that in either one she'd be the same as she was here—a lookout, someone set off apart, a necessary part of the picture but not the integral one.

Quietly, in her spare moments, she went through her old mail, crumpling letters to be destroyed and packing them in paper bags; saving a few. She packed her books in cartons and left out only the clothes she would need.

And she listened to weather reports like a racer listening to the starting gun. Now that she was leaving she might as well be on her way to the next stop.

The first storm veered up through Canada, and she settled back for another wait. This time she checked her resources. Money had been deposited in her account for the books and furniture. She could take a vacation if she wanted to.

But what has this been except a vacation? she asked.

The next mail was brought up by a tower maintenance man who checked to see if anything was needed at the tower to protect it through harsh winter storms. Tess, eager for talk, found him most uncommunicative. He had work to do, and by a few expressive grunts indicated that chatting with lonely lookouts wasn't part of it.

It was strange. As long as she'd known she must look ahead to weeks of living alone, she hadn't minded too much. But now she was marking days, waiting for fall storms to bring her release. She thought she couldn't stand the loneliness.

Turned back upon her own company, Tess carried her mail to the tower, sifted through and brought out a letter from Matt. And for the first time in months she felt a singing upswing in her heart. She hadn't heard from him for weeks; now this bulky letter.

She read it in snatches as she made her rounds. When evening came, sunset writing a golden script on a cold sky, she stood and thought of Matt; the change in him, in her and in Al.

Matt hadn't gone to a tower or worked in the woods. He had taken a canoe and worked his way down-river by paddle, camped on lonely river sands at night. He was free of telephones, business and social demands and had, he said, "time for more than surface thinking."

He'd written, "I've been so busy climbing a ladder I haven't taken time to look on either side of it or where I'd be when I reached the top."

He'd spoken about the Palmer house. "In one sense you were right. I did look upon it as a goal, but you were wrong in thinking it a material goal. It was like a talisman, a lucky charm. I felt if I had it near I could be more like the men who'd lived in it."

Then she came to the part she loved the most. "I'm glad you ran away from our wedding, Tess. It wasn't that I didn't love you, but I did have that love all mixed up with the Palmers. Now that I can see you apart from them, away from the house, I find you lovelier and more desirable than ever. Give me a chance to show that this winter, perhaps by spring, I can prove my case—"

It was peculiar. Matt and Al had found their answers but she who had deliberately sought an answer to her question had been the one to fail.

Why? Perhaps she hadn't framed the question clearly, hadn't known exactly what she'd wanted answered.

Night came early these days, and gratefully she went into the warm cabin, automatically turning on her radio for the evening news. In another moment she was staring at the small box in alarm, not knowing why.

"—escaped from the guards taking him before an examining board. It has been the policy of the prison to refrain from using handcuffs at public hearings. Decker Monrove apparently knew this and planned his escape accordingly.

An alarm has been broadcast to five states, as it is believed he will try to cross a state border.

Monrove's mother scoffs at his leaving the state. She declares he will seek shelter in the woods he knows.

Decker's wife, Mona Monrove, could not be reached for questioning. Neighbors caring for the children said Decker's wife had gone to the valley to work in the potato fields.

Police commented that one of the largest harvests is being carried on within a few miles of the penitentiary."

Tess turned out the light, went back to the catwalk and looked down into the black forests where Decker would feel safe.

CHAPTER 11

Tess awakened to clear frosty skies. Below, the mountains had a mottled appearance. Deciduous trees now flaunted their difference in scarlet and gold.

She thought instantly of Decker. If he had reached the woods he'd have spent a cold night. Or would he? Mona with her shrewd grey eyes would have prepared some means of sheltering him if they had made contact.

Why do they try? she wondered as she prepared her breakfast. They never win. If they're not captured they are shot.

Yet not always. There was always the percentage that got away. You read of someone being found or willingly giving himself up twenty or thirty years later. Often they had lived respectable lives in the interim.

She supposed this hope lay in the heart of each: that he would be one who got away and stayed away.

And of course Mona, a "fruit gypsy," would know every camping spot from one border to the other.

Tess listened to the morning news. She learned now that three men had broken away at the same time. One had been captured within the halls; one had been found that night on the river's edge looking for a boat to float downstream and break his tracks. Monrove had simply vanished.

Tess paced the catwalk restlessly that day. The woods were open again, permanent smokes showing blue plumes. The extreme danger period was over, but there was still fire danger.

Now that her time here was nearly over, she felt caged, trapped, wanted to be out and into whatever life lay immediately ahead.

Imagine, came an inner voice, being caged for a long term in prison.

She could leave if she had to. She could also run down the steps and walk in the woods or down the road and have no one standing above her with a gun.

Above all, she had no miserable sense of guilt and need of rationalization riding her shoulders.

The noon news reported that a bundle of prison clothing had been found on the highway leading north. It had been identified as Decker Monrove's, and was presumed to have been thrown from a car. However, as it had been damp with night dew, it was estimated Monrove had gotten rid of it the night before.

This, said the authorities, indicated a planned escape with someone on the outside waiting. It was not Mrs. Monrove, the report declared. She was back in the potato field and had explained her absence satisfactorily.

Tess knew what that meant. They had accepted her story that she'd drawn some money, gone shopping for the children, taken their new clothes down to them, then returned to work. They had, they reported, checked each step.

Privately they had figured the time involved. She had shopped forty miles north of the scene of escape at an hour that almost coincided with it. She had then driven southwest to her home, then directly east and then north, back to the potato fields.

From her lookout tower Tess followed the general route Mona Monrove had taken, then bisected it with an imaginary line. If some other person, say one of Mona's brothers, had been waiting for Decker, he could have cut across at an angle and met her on the southwest highway. Decker could have transferred to Mona's car, the brother returning to dispose of the clothing at a spot they'd previously chosen.

Mona's excuse was perfect. She'd said their oldest child was entering school, "and didn't have a decent rag to her name."

Idly Tess went to look at the big map which carried not only her district but the one to the west. She knew the name of the logging town where Mona had been living. Now, with surprise, she found it was almost due west.

"If she'd taken a straight route back to the valley," she reasoned, tracing highways, "she'd have come right along that highway at the foot of the north bluff."

She thought then of the ledge the city boy had tried to climb on a dare, and discounted that.

Decker was too good a woodsman.

But where would he go?

The answer was simple: some abandoned cabin he'd have known about. And Mona or whoever was working with her would have stocked it. He would plan to lie low there until the heat was off, then make a carefully planned getaway out of the state.

Tess stood on the west side of the lookout and stared at the hills, at ridge after ridge of them, at peaks and valleys, at canyons.

Why should I care? she asked herself.

Just because we were in high school together, or because he mowed our lawns one summer and I'd sit hunched up on the steps and talk to him, why am I so concerned about his escape?

She'd pretend he was a total stranger and rid her mind of him.

If he were, she reasoned, I'd watch for smoke from a cabin chimney. Now if the cabin were in the open it would rise straight up or slant to the wind. If it were under trees it would flatten and seep up.

And if I had the sense given little green geese I'd know no fugitive would build a fire in a cabin or any place else in the daytime. Not if he knew anything at all about the woods and lookouts.

She thought of a lookout reporting a smoke, someone from headquarters going in to investigate and being met with a fusillage. Mona would have seen that Decker had firearms of some kind.

And here she was back to Decker again.

The evening newscasts confirmed her hunch. It was believed Decker Monrove had managed to cross the valley and get into the mountains he knew.

That night she looked down on the blackness of the forests and wondered. What was it like to be hunted?

It was growing cold now. The stars seemed to have been polished with frost and were no longer friendly.

"Anticlimax," she said aloud, going into the cabin. "That's what I'm suffering from. I should light my little lamp and read myself to sleep."

Only she didn't want to light a lamp. For some reason, she felt her mountain peak privacy had been invaded. And with nothing between her and the night but glass walls, she'd keep those dark.

Al King came the next morning, and the moment he was out of the truck Tess was down the stairs wanting, for some reason, to throw herself in his arms.

"Al, I haven't talked to anyone but myself for so long I feel like a chipmunk."

"Ha," he jeered, "end of the season twirps. They get some people. Like being dressed for a date too early."

"It is, exactly," Tess cried, "as though you were all dressed up and couldn't go about your usual chores; just had to wait for the right moment."

"Shall we go up?"

Tess, in the riding breeches and jodhpurs she'd found best for this climb, went quickly before him and, once up, removed her sweater. "I tried flannel shirts, but the temperature up here is too changeable. What's new below?"

"More anticlimax," he reported. They'd lost part of their crew to college, part of their lookouts to schools. Everyone was waiting for the first heavy rains, and they all seemed to have destinies in another direction. Some stopped off to the south, others were flying by overhead to Canada.

There was no mail, but he'd brought the morning newspaper.

"You read it. I'll take a look for you."

Willingly Tess unrolled the paper and then gave a little cry. "Al, this can't be Decker."

"Not the one you know," he agreed, and went on out, leaving her to read.

But she remained staring at the photograph which had been blown up to a two-column cut. It had been taken, she learned in the caption, at the time of the accident which had put him in the infirmary.

Across the top was printed in large letters:

HAVE YOU SEEN THIS MAN?

Underneath, it advised anyone seeing him to call the nearest police headquarters. It warned against any attempt at capture by an unarmed citizen.

Al's movement caused Tess to look up. He'd walked to the west and was now standing at the southwest corner and had lifted binoculars to his eyes. He hadn't bothered to take a check look in any other direction.

"I wonder who he thinks he's fooling," she whispered.

She turned back to the newspaper picture, but now that she knew who it was, found it difficult to see it as she had at first. Superimposed upon the printed photograph were her memories of Monrove. He wasn't this vicious-looking "animal;" she said the word because nothing else seemed to fit.

She wondered how the photograph chanced to be taken. Ordinary difficulties within prison walls were not publicized. Possibly a chance shot of a news photographer in on other business.

Tess read the news story. It was mostly rehash; little more had been learned, at least for publication, than she had heard over the air.

On an inside page were pictures of Mona Monrove, of Mrs. Dess Monrove, Decker's mother, and a small group photograph of the children taken at the time of Decker's trial. Matt had had them brought into court, hoping they would make some impression on the jury.

Tess thought these children weren't going to have much more of a chance than Decker had had. Then she remembered Juxton. He'd had everything a normal boy could want, yet he'd stolen more, much more than Decker.

She wondered if Juxton could look as Decker looked in that photograph if he were cornered.

Restlessly she rose and walked out to King. "Expecting fireworks to the southwest?" she inquired.

"Could be. Crew going in there this afternoon. They'll start cutting tomorrow."

Then maybe she'd been wrong. However, "in there" covered an awful lot of territory from a binocular point of view.

"Wish it would rain," he continued irrelevantly.

He said he couldn't stay to lunch, but he seemed in no hurry to leave.

"Your other boy friend phoned this morning," he finally blurted. "Matt Seares. He's worried about you."

"About me? Why?"

"Monrove knows you're in this lookout."

"Oh?"

"Seems he wanted to talk to you when his appeal was denied. He said the old Judge's daughter could do something for him. Seares finally told him you were stuck in a lookout for the summer and wouldn't be free to leave before the fire season was over. Monrove could understand that, but he was interested. He'd logged around these hills and wanted to know which one you were in, and Seares saw no reason for not telling him."

"So what?" Tess asked.

"Good gosh, Tess, don't you understand? He could come up here, especially if he needed supplies. He'd figure you'd help him out. He'd feel safe. He'd know you wouldn't turn him in."

"Oh, no," breathed Tess.

"You wouldn't or wouldn't refrain from it?"

"I didn't mean either," Tess replied absently. "I only thought what a horrible position to be in, to have to make a choice. Oh, but then he wouldn't come up here," she began. "He knows this whole area, Al. He would know they were cutting up through here. And he'd be working farther south into the Siskiyous, toward the state line."

"And if he's as cunning as they say he is, he'd figure that's what the police would think. They believe he's looking for some point of contact with his wife. If he's going to travel, he's going to need money. He can't get it the hard way without the police picking up his trail. She's been picking up a tidy sum with potatoes. She's a fast worker.

"Of course she'd know she was being watched."

A call came from headquarters and Al had to leave, but he went reluctantly.

"Remember this isn't the Monrove you knew in school," he repeated. "Don't go wandering over the mountain top because you're getting bored. I know the check call would alert us, but it wouldn't help to have you held hostage. And, Tess, report anything in your area that looks unusual. Don't let sentiment ruin your record as a lookout."

"Do you forget I'm a judge's daughter?" she asked.

"Don't you," he returned gravely. "I'd hate to start off for the New Hebrides without you."

"Men!" said Tess savagely when he'd left. "First I'm a piece of furniture in my own home.

Now I'm someone with a note book to take down observations. I wonder if any of them think of me as a person. I wonder what I'd do if they thought of me without their blessed professions in the foregrounds."

At twilight she thought of earlier generations, of an era when romance was not ridiculed. It must have been wonderful to have been a girl in such a generation, to have been considered fragile and so desirable men would fight duels over her.

She thought of Matt and Al and decided if they knew a choice had to be made between them, each would draw up a prospectus and expect her to evaluate the potential benefits of being married to one or the other.

Maybe it was her own fault. Lookouts weren't fragile. They could live alone without yelling for some male to rescue them from imagined dangers. They were a healthy lot. They also came equipped with an alert set of brains. As for looks—

Even in the twilight, the small mirror Tess had brought gave little reassurance. Al had brought up a barber kit long ago, but he hadn't brought up any dexterity to go with it.

"The first thing I'll do when I'm down is to go to a beauty shop. Correction," she cut in quickly. "The first move is to a hotel room with large bathtub attached. There I shall soak for hours."

One thing about being a lookout lady—by the end of the season one really appreciated all of the little home comforts previously taken for granted.

She listened to the late newscast, but it told so little she believed the police were being cagy about what they gave out, feeling Monrove might have access to a radio.

There'd been reports that he had been seen in a hundred places as many miles apart, all at the same time. Each had been investigated.

The only thing encouraging about the weather report was that the forecaster was usually wrong. The low, he said, was still lowering off the north California coast, held back by a strong high pressure.

Tess yawned to bed. At least the farmers could get their nut harvest in without scrambling around in the mud.

It was pitch black when she awakened. For a

long time she lay stiff with alarm, trying to remember what had brought her up out of deep
slumber.

"A shot," she whispered. "The crack of a
rifle."

The illuminated dial of her clock indicated
the shot had been at two-thirty exactly. But why
would there be any necessity of shooting at that
hour?

Someone spotlight hunting? Surely not up
here. Most hunters on that illegal venture tried
brushy side roads where they could make a quick
getaway in a car.

But if a man were hungry?

Reluctantly she slipped into a dark robe and
slippers and eased out onto the catwalk. Instinc-
tively, she moved around away from the door
to the southwest corner.

Who said nights were black velvet? She
shivered. This one is satin, cold, slinky—

The bare ground below the lookout was a
shade less dark than the hills. The washhouse
squatted like a black gnome. Was she imagining
something moving around it; a bear, some
humped over creature, a bulky shadow?

CHAPTER 12

A bear, Tess decided. She'd seen tracks around the spring one day, and as the dry season had checked the flow, one had wallowed in the mud. And of course, that shot she thought she'd heard had been a limb breaking. They did often, with changes of temperature, and went off like a charge.

When the sun came up the phantasmagoria of the night would vanish. Sun? Tess looked up and wanted to sing. There were no stars. Imagine being happy about that. But she was. She might return to a lookout another year, eager to be alone with the sky, but right now she was yearning for a break in the weather which would put her down with a telephone at her elbow.

Of course she had the radio, but she was blessed if she were going to make a fool of herself by reporting illusory sights and sounds.

Sleep wouldn't return. Tess thought of her electric hot pad tucked miles away, and huddled in bed.

The daughter of a judge, when she was an only child and motherless, was taught to think and to reason. It became a habit. You took a conclusion and worked back to the cause.

Tess took an imaginary rifle shot and worked back. If the shot had not been fired at a deer, why would it have been discharged?

"Signal," muttered Tess. For whom? Were the police in the hills?

"All right, face it," she told herself. "Work from the premise that Decker is near. He could be hungry and kill a deer. Or, if it were a signal, Mona or one of Mona's brothers?"

Al had said the police believed Decker was trying to establish contact with his wife. Mona had been purportedly shopping at the time of Decker's escape. She'd said she'd been shopping for school clothes. She could have shopped elsewhere for Decker, and have left the clothes and a message saying she'd join him on a given date at a given place.

A hiding spot in the woods couldn't be pin-pointed, but if it were above human habitation with no one but a lookout within earshot. And if he expected her this particular day, "Saturday, pay day," whispered Tess, a single shot at a certain hour would give Mona the general direction in which to travel.

Why my lookout? Tess inquired of the darkness.

They'd have had to make their plans weeks earlier with a guard listening. There'd be nothing suspicious to those ears if the two were to discuss an old school friend taking a lookout on Phantom Peak. Their eyes could have conveyed the rest of the message.

So far so good. But where would they go from here?

In the darkness Tess brought up a mental picture of her map and saw the wisdom of such a plan. They could travel a ridge route for many miles without meeting civilization. It would be tough going, but the hunted accepted that, and Decker, a woodsman, would be at home. Mona had had a chilhood spent roughing it.

They'd have to work their way across the state line, but that could be done. Inspection stations were found only on the main highways. If they could get through before snowfall, there were roads through the Siskiyous.

Once over, they stood a fair chance of finding a home.

But what of the children?

Mona's family would absorb them. That family moved up and down the coast and back and forth across the country so often, nothing was thought of it. And if they were made court wards? They'd hardly be taken from a maternal grandmother. Later, the family might unite.

I can certainly work up a case, Tess thought, wondering if morning would ever come.

It would take many people to see Decker through. But there was a lot of sympathy for him. Not that he hadn't been guilty of something they'd never have done, but because in the same court a man guilty of so much more, in their eyes, had been given probation.

Matt had written in one letter that Decker's former co-workers were getting up a "purse" for the children.

"And in the morning," she said finally, "I'll go down and find a brother bruin has been giving my washhouse an inspection, in consideration of using it as winter hibernation quarters."

Morning finally arrived. Tess wakened groggily and glanced automatically at the sky. It was overcast, with white clouds like fancy icing.

She put some oatmeal on to cook, shaking the box of the last flakes, tossed in the few remaining raisins and thought that the sky better mean what it said, or she'd be out of groceries.

She made her first check call after a quick survey of her domain. Then, before heading down to the washroom, she stood looking and listening.

A soft wind in the trees, but that was all. Not even a cub bear in the foreground. She'd been having hallucinations the previous night. Al's message from Matt had made her more nervous than she'd realized.

She found nothing suspicious any place around the building and, relieved, returned to breakfast.

She'd savor every moment of this day; her

last before plunging back into life.

On her second check look she discovered quite a smoke bank to the north, well out of her district but worth a call on general principles.

"Brush fire. Started from a rancher burning stubble, and it got away," the dispatcher told her. "We're pretty busy here this morning. How are things up there? Hear anything during the night?"

Tess thought quickly. If things were busy at headquarters, she wasn't going to report any alarms.

"N-no," she said, unaware of the uncertain note until the dispatcher questioned her.

"Oh, I just thought I saw a bear trying to get into the washroom about two-forty-five this morning. He humped off down into the woods."

She heard a call coming in on the dispatcher's board and found herself cut off.

She would like to mark up a season without any false alarms. Besides, she was in the fire lookout business, not in police enforcement.

The mid-morning news carried a story on the brush fire. The farmer whose stubble had burned swore he'd not set it. Fire marshals from the rural districts reported a fire bug at work. Fires had been set at intervals along a mile stretch of brush, most of it edging farmlands. It was racing up into a reforestation area.

Tess went about her business, wondering what really adequate punishment could be meted out to fire bugs. What this country needs, she decided, is a revision of laws; laws with teeth in them and men on the bench to see those teeth closed tight.

Southwest, she lifted her face to the breeze, a rain wind. Evidently that low in the Pacific had sneaked in under the high pressure. The question before the lookout now was: would it strike soon enough to blanket the fire and release the equipment so someone would be free to come after her?

It was strange. Yesterday she'd thought she would be remaining several additional days and had accepted it cheerfully. Today she felt she could not face another night.

By four o'clock she knew she'd have to. The rain wouldn't start now until twilight.

I'll enjoy it, she insisted stoutly, I'll listen to the rain on the roof. There's enough gas for a good fire, and I'll read. All right, so I have to unpack to find a book.

She'd also have to make biscuits. Well, another year she'd learn to keep more food on hand until she was sure of the date she'd be leaving.

The final check call came early these autumn days. This time central lookout broke from ritual. "Seen anymore bears?"

"No," Tess reported.

"If you see any of the genus homo variety, add the call letters GM."

"Check," agreed Tess.

"Been down yet? Then go. I'll give you another check call in half an hour."

She had switched off before Tess could ask why the concern. However, as she'd mentioned bears, the dispatcher had probably relayed the message to her and, being busy with fires, let her handle it.

Tess descended into the blue twilight as warily as into a pool of ice water. The area around the tower was clear of trees, but dark shadows lurked on the perimeter. And each was a potential danger.

Tess remembered nights when she had been

restless and come down to pace cheerfully back and forth and wondered at her sudden apprehension.

When she'd scuttled back up the steps and the steel door had dropped bolted into place, she found she was perspiring.

She missed the six o'clock news. The check-call came, and this time central lookout had more to say.

"We've been double checking all lookouts. Use your imagination. No danger, but stay put until after the first morning check call."

"Roger," agreed Tess heartily.

She felt she'd been using her imagination all day and there was none left over. But if all lookouts were being double-checked, that meant that genus homo was reported in this area.

Little prickles of fear ran up and down Tess's spine until she cried, "Oh, for goodness sake, girl, remember Decker as you knew him. Remember that day you took lemonade and cookies out to him when he was mowing the lawn, and how you sat and talked together?"

What had they talked about? Decker was just outgrowing his shyness, replacing it with defiance, and between long gulps of lemonade, he told her what he planned to do. He wasn't sure just what, but it was going to be the most.

Of course, Tess thought now, it would have to be the most of whatever it was to make up for the least he'd always had.

Having brought Decker Monrove, escaped convict, into focus as Decker the boy who mowed the lawn, Tess felt considerably better. She'd been influenced by radio bulletins to think of him as some weird and dangerous person.

Nevertheless, she waited until her lights were out before venturing out on the catwalk for some final deep breaths of damp air.

She was a little alarmed once. She could smell smoke. And then she thought, naturally. There'd been a fire that day; some of the smoke had been caught in a counter current and drifted her way.

"Onions frying," she said. "Ridiculous. I can smell violets if I think about them long enough."

By sheer will power she remained awake until the ten o'clock news, and then sat tensely listening to every word.

"—believed to have set the brush fires to draw police as well as fire equipment to that area and away from the hill roads he expected to use as a getaway—"

It would be a smart idea, she conceded. Judging from the location of the fire, there'd be an awful traffic jam of coast and valley-bound cars and trucks. There'd be minor accidents. And with the fire district busy—

Except that Decker wouldn't set fires. He'd spent too many years in the woods. That is, the old Decker wouldn't.

And if he had, he wasn't any place near Phantom Peak. And she was safe. She was high on a tower that nothing but a plane could destroy. And if what she heard on the roof of that tower was true, she'd be down and away from the peak before he and Mona could set up housekeeping anywhere near.

When she awakened in the morning she found a steady drizzle had set in. Heavy rain would come later, and sometime today she would go down from Phantom Peak.

"Biscuits again," she said gayly. "Tomorrow morning, toast and trimmings in a hotel or café. I can't possibly decide on an apartment and move in that soon."

Closing the oven door, she took an automatic glance outside and, inured to routine, went out. And now she did smell smoke right through the drizzle and found it due west, somewhere below and beyond the washhouse.

Her reaction was instinctive. There was smoke to be reported. Let the dispatcher decide whether the rain was heavy enough to control it.

She wheeled, and below a voice rang out, "Tess!"

Mona Monrove had come out from under the tower and stood now at an angle away from it, a rifle nonchalantly under her arm, a rifle which could swing up swiftly.

"You seen Decker?"

"Good heavens no." Mentally Tess computed the time it would take her to get around the corner and into the door at the northeast corner.

"I've got to find him. What's the radio say? Where they hunting him now?"

So that was it. Something had delayed them. Now they had to have news of the search because, of course, Decker was with her, close by, listening. A woman, declared Tess's purely feminine logic, wouldn't bother with onions in a hamburger for herself at such a time. A woman cooking for a man she loved would add that extra touch.

"I don't know, Mona," Tess answered evenly. "I haven't a short wave I can use for police calls. I haven't listened to the morning news."

"Then last night, about the fire—"

That meant one of two things. Either they were in some way responsible for the fire or— and she shivered a little—one of them had climbed to within hearing distance of the radio inside the tower. And she kept it tuned low.

Tess repeated what the newscaster had said and Mona watched, not moving.

"I want to come up," she stated when Tess was through. "I can listen to all the bulletins and maybe find him. I want him to give himself up. Decker says he can trust you, Tess. Something about your father—"

Al had said the one thing they didn't want was her being held as hostage. Mona, once in the tower, could have other weapons, and Mona and Decker together there could hold out for a little while.

"This is government property. I can't let you

up. Mona, let me run in and get a coat. I've biscuits in the oven."

The rifle was up now. "And get on that radio? Not on your life. Maybe Deck trusts you. I don't."

Tess was alert now, playing for time. She was keenly aware of her isolation, of the cold wet wind, the mist-shrouded trees and, above all, of the girl below.

"Why should I radio anyone?" she asked reasonably. "The police aren't looking for you. If I go in I can catch the morning news."

"How do I know you'll tell me the truth?"

"Come up the ladder and listen."

Mona waited, undecided, and Tess spoke again. "Central lookout is due to call. If I'm not in there to answer back, she'll call headquarters and someone will come up to investigate."

"Yeah? We can take care of them."

They could. Or could they? After the cryptic words of central lookout last night, wouldn't anyone approaching be wary? Al, for instance?

And Mona had said we. Interesting, now that she knew what she was facing, Tess felt relieved.

She explained to Mona about check-calls. Tess

could sense how it disturbed Mona Monrove, and upset whatever plans they'd made.

"When this central calls you could say I'm here. Then what?"

"When she calls I only give the call letters."

"Yeah?" came the derisive question.

"Five-five-five GH zero minus."

Now how had she thought that up so quickly? Genus homo at zero would mean with her, minus would surely mean just below the tower.

"Okay," Mona agreed then. "Wait a minute. We figured. There's not a spot in that glass cage we can't hit. Deck's got you covered. I'm comin' up the steps. If you let one peep out of you, I signal and he lets go. Understand?"

CHAPTER 13

There was one spot on the north side of the fire finder where they couldn't reach her. She needn't reply to central lookout's check call. Someone would come up.

If she put her message over it would mean the state police would close in. With Mona and Decker both armed, it meant someone would be killed.

Yet if she didn't report, what then? They'd get away, and perhaps some place south, when supplies ran out, some lonely farmhouse would be invaded and some member of the family, usually the father, the provider who'd fight, would be killed. That was the pattern of escaped convicts. It rarely deviated.

Matt had said earlier that Decker was a potential killer, that therein lay the difference between his minor theft and Juxton's grand theft.

Even as she was thinking these things, Tess was sweeping into the cabin, bending to take the highly browned biscuits from the oven. Mona, the housewife, would recognize the sound of oven doors, would know she'd been truthful in one thing.

In ten minutes central lookout would call in. The first newscast came at almost the same time.

Dad, she appealed, what should I do? What's the right thing to do?

Judge Palmer had said the nation's laws were its framework, its bone structure. An infraction was a fracture, and if not corrected it weakened the whole structure, the whole body.

Decker had been out of work and his children hungry, he'd said in his defense. But thousands of loggers had been out of work and had managed to provide for their families, meager though that provision was.

Mona's voice, slyly friendly, came from below the trap door. "I sure could use one of those biscuits."

"Fine. I'll butter some and drop them over the north side."

"I'd have to climb these blasted steps again. Why can't you slip them through a crack in the trap door?"

"Government property," droned Tess.

She could recapitulate now. For some reason they'd been unable to get away. There could be nothing as safe as her tower. If they could barricade themselves inside they could not only hold out, but pick off intruders.

"You got any medicine and stuff up there?" Mona asked. "You can throw it over the side, only I don't know nothin' about fixing a guy up. I never took first aid. You did. I remember you helping the civil defense guy at high."

Now why hadn't they come to her with this story first; let her see Decker needed help? She'd have quick to respond, to help, and then they could have taken her, taken the tower.

"What kind of medicine, Mona? I'm about out of everything. What's wrong with Decker?"

"He got some ribs busted when he first got sent up. Other day he tripped on a vine and knocked 'em out again; can't breathe good. He says they need tape. Then that tendon he hurt at school let go. If you could come down and fix it up, maybe he could walk enough to get out of here."

Mona didn't need to add, "I'm leveling, Tess." Tess knew it was true. It all fitted in now. The planned escape had worked out until Decker had tripped on a ground vine. Phantom had come into the picture only as a place to meet, well away from people.

It was after they had met they had laid new plans. Decker would know about weekly supplies. They'd wait until someone had been up, then try to get in. That would give them six days for his injuries to heal. They might even have planned to take her with them when they left; then turn her loose some place where it would take time to make her way out.

"I can tear up a sheet," she was answering, "but I've only quarter-inch adhesive tape left. What he needs is X-rays, Mona. On which side were the ribs broken?"

"Left."

"There could be pressure on his heart."

"I'm not scarin'," Mona stated emphatically,

"and don't try no goody talk on me. Decker's not givin' up."

Tess looked at the clock for the tenth time. Would it never reach the mark?

When it did and the call came through, she jumped as though a shot had been fired. And she stood now where Decker could, if rightly placed, be aiming at her, with Mona below, listening, ready to signal him. Hadn't they realized that a shot would be heard?

As soon as central lookout's voice stopped, Tess was ready.

"Five-five-five GH zero minus," she droned.

"Check?" came unexpectedly.

Here was her chance. "Double check."

"Rog . . . *er*!"

There, she'd done it—called in the state game hunter; no, no, the State Police. And they'd come in knowing their prey was double.

"When's the news?" asked Mona.

"Right now."

The first news story on national affairs was over. International news came on then at the end of the period.

"The manhunt for escaped Decker Monrove

continues. It is believed now he is heading south, taking advantage of yesterday's fire in the south central area, set, it has been proven, by a brother-in-law, Seth Sale, who authorities believe also assisted in his escape.

There was the usual description, and that was all.

"Didn't say nothin' about me at all," Mona commented.

"Seth won't squeal," she declared, but there was a lack of conviction in her voice.

Fifteen minutes had passed since the check-call. Tess made coffee, tried to eat a biscuit, but it stuck in her throat. Her whole mind now must be given to making the capture as easy as possible. But how could she, up here, do anything at all?

Another fifteen minutes and the radio sounded.

"Calling five-five-five GH," said central look-out. "Tillicum reports a smoke at 365. Please confirm double zero minus."

Tess gave thanks it was Mona and not Decker within earshot. He'd have caught that zero minus.

"Will check and call back."

"Mona," Tess said, "Tillicum Lookout to the west is reporting a smoke, a fire here in my area. I have to locate it and call back."

"What do you say when you do?" she demanded suspiciously.

"I locate it on the fire finder and give the degrees; just numbers."

"You don't give it right, understand? We don't want no fire outfit up here now."

"Probably the fire you built for breakfast," Tess soothed.

"You seen that?" cried Mona. "Say, is that why you didn't come down?"

She'd been right about that, Tess thought. They had counted on catching her on the ground.

Now to find another cover.

"I'll report a mist at that location. Have to," she insisted at Mona's protest. "It has to double check with Tillicum's report."

She had to find more than the smoke in that quick look. She had to find Decker's hideout so the men coming in need not be taken by surprise.

One thing about spending days in a given place, days spent in searching horizons and near landscapes—one learned every bump on the earth's surface. Tess knew and found only such bumps as she knew. Decker was nowhere in sight.

Decker, thought Tess, is on the lam. Which way had he gone and how far could he get if he were really injured she couldn't guess.

"Make it snappy," ordered Mona irritably.

Tess continued her even pace around the cabin. And then she saw him. There was wisdom in his choice, and extreme danger. He was easing toward the north slide, and just as there had been spots below where a man might climb, so there were ledges above where a man might creep along.

Tess called central lookout to report a mist disappearing at 365, blown approximately 158, then added F zero minus.

"I'm gettin' knots in my legs standin' here," Mona announced. "I'm goin' down. But I can hear you, and Decker is watchin'."

Feeling free now, Tess slipped off her shoes and slipped on sneakers. She moved slowly around, looking carefully into the brush.

She saw Mona slip out from under the tower

and start for the northeast, and as she reached the underbrush a blue-grey arm reached out to clamp a hand over her mouth, a second blue-grey clad figure appeared and bound her arms. Then they carried her kicking out of vision.

Tess knew now her information had been relayed to police car radios just out of sound reach, and the men, acting on the information, had come in toward the direction Decker had taken.

She could see him from the tower now. Here a lip of the cliff had broken off and Decker was standing on the rock which had caught on a ledge, doubled over, unquestionably drawing labored breaths.

Compassion and irritation swept over Tess. Why had he been so stupid? All of his carefully laid plans had been ruined by a vine, and he had no alternate plans ready. They'd tried to bluff her and, failing, he'd taken a desperate measure.

Swiftly she moved around now, aware of other figures closing in on her knoll. She had signaled Decker's location, but they were not moving forward.

Here was the reason. A man, his hands out to

show he was unarmed, was coming up the hill, moving toward the lip of the bluff; a man in business clothes.

Now his voice came up to Tess clearly.

"Decker, this is Matt Seares. I'm not armed. Deck, I want to talk to you."

Tess ran to the northeast corner of the catwalk. "Matt, don't. He won't believe you. Decker doesn't believe himself, so he can't believe you."

A watery sun had come out briefly. Bushes and tree tops sparkled with raindrops. Across the gorge the walls of the mountain were deep blue, and Matt moved toward them without looking back.

"Decker, I'm coming as your attorney. I've fought for you."

"Yeah," Decker spoke for the first time, "but not like you fought for Juxton. He was one o' your kind."

"Matt," Tess called again, "Decker's hurt. He's in pain and has fever." Maybe that would give him an idea of an irrational brain.

But was it irrational to throw Juxton at him? Hadn't she?

Matt's voice was fainter now. He was talking against time, telling Decker he'd be in a hospital and eased of his pain in a short time. Later they'd find some occupational therapy and he'd come out with a fine profession that would support his family.

"I'd sooner die than go back!" came the bitter reply.

The state Police were moving in now, a grey-blue background for Matt, yet out of sight of Decker.

Matt was silhouetted against the hill. When he disappeared, a sound ricocheted in the canyon below.

Frantic, Tess ran to the trap door and heard the dispatcher's voice say, "stand by."

She raced back and found police around the lip of the slide, heard motors and found forestry trucks moving in from the south.

What had she done wrong? Should she have warned Mona first, told her to get Decker away? Or should she have pretended all was well at Phantom Peak when she talked to central look-out?

Decker had come there because of her. She

had been something familiar, and perhaps he'd counted on her as he'd counted on her father when times were lean and he'd come asking for work to make enough for what he had to have. He had always found it and been given the dignity of earning it.

Suddenly she saw Al running toward the gorge lip with a canvas. For Matt or Decker? There'd been only one shot. Why couldn't she see that one vital spot?

Tess heard her call signal.

"I don't know," she reported. "I can't see. Matt went over the lip of the bluff just as there was a shot. I don't know whether he was shot or if the police fired at Decker. Al took a canvas. Oh, and there's someone with rope and first aid."

"Then," came the calm voice, "the shot wasn't fatal or first aid wouldn't be needed."

"Of course," came a great sigh.

"We'll have an ambulance ready. Better check."

For a few moments she couldn't see who was in the canvas sling. There were so many around helping. And then they passed close to the tower and she saw it was Matt. But why had they been so long?

Al looked up. "Not too bad, Tess. Decker got him in the shoulder. He pitched forward, broke his leg; just a fracture, we hope." And then he called back. "The boys are bringing you down. Pack up!"

"What happened to Decker?" she called.

"Why, he—" the first one began; then an older man took up the reply.

"He got away from us. Went over the side. We'll get him from down there. We have men posted along the canyon highway."

CHAPTER 14

When everything was ready and the tower as clean as she could leave it, Tess went for her last check-look. But there was nothing to see, nothing at all. The rain clouds had closed down as closely as the shutters would be in a little while.

Phantom Peak was closed for the season.

It was queer how Decker's and Juxton's trials had brought her out here, seeking a high place to think things out. There'd always been an incompleteness about the Monrove case. Now, like Phantom Peak, it too was closed.

The boys who came after her were full of talk. Al King had gone on to the hospital with Matt Seares. They found the "whole deal" terrifically exciting and asked innumerable questions. And Tess answered those she could.

At headquarters she found the usual understanding. They knew she didn't want to talk about what had happened that day. She'd be back, she promised, in a day or two. And no, she hadn't an address yet, but general delivery at her home town would reach her.

Tess had thought she was alone in the lookout on Phantom Peak. Now, driving along the highway, trying to hold her own steady pace against the erratic plunges of other cars, she wondered.

Through the arc of windshield wipers she saw the city lights and swung east. She'd telephone the hospital. But she drove straight to it and, unaware of how she looked in breeches, her last clean and most unattractive flannel shirt, a scarf over her head, raced in.

"Matt Seares," repeated the reception clerk, and turned as the switchboard operator spoke. "If that's Miss Palmer, she's to go straight up."

Going up in the elevator, Tess found her nerves bunched into tight knots of worry. Matt must be worse than they'd realized at first.

Al King was waiting for her on the fifth floor,

and Tess wanted to lean against his arm in relief.

"Nothing dangerous," he assured her. "The doctors thought a visit from you would be better than more sedation. It seems he has things on his mind."

Al walked in with her, and Tess, hands clenched, arms held stiffly at her sides, moved toward the bed where Matt lay in traction, one shoulder twice its normal size.

"Isn't she beautiful?" Matt demanded sleepily of Al.

Tess looked at the nurse and mouthed, "Delirious," and the nurse, smiling, shook her head and mouthed back, "No." Aloud she said, "No more than three minutes," and, taking Al with her, left.

"Had to talk to you. Tess, I killed Decker. No," Matt moved his head restlessly, "not with a gun. He'd have taken his sentence like a man if the Juxton jury hadn't brought in a plea for leniency. I did that. One smart lawyer, Tess.

"You saw it. Took me a long time to figure that it wasn't the Monrove verdict, but the discrepancy between the two verdicts that had upset you. You were right.

"Tess, too many of us lawyers think more of winning a case than of the case. Been too ambitious, Tess. Still am, but in a different way. See law now as your father saw it; just, impartial. Not the conviction of the minority, but the protection of the majority.

"Wanted to tell you before you went away."

Tess swallowed the lump in her throat. "But, Matt, I'm only going to a hotel to put myself in to soak. In a tub, I mean. Tomorrow I'll look for an apartment. That way I can visit you every day.

"How long are you in for?" she asked.

Matt laughed and groaned. "Doc handed down a verdict of thirty days; then I'll be out on good behavior."

"Good. I'll have a thirty day vacation. Then I must look for a home and a job."

"How about Al?"

The nurse came in, saying their visiting time was up, and Tess turned to her. "May I kiss him?"

The nurse looked judicious. "Hm, fracture of the right leg, left shoulder wound. I think if you were to approach from the right—"

Left shoulder wound. A left shoulder was so close to the heart. Tess left tears as well as a kiss.

"Tess," Matt's eyes cleared of their drowsiness, "about that home and that job. Nurse, big envelope in my coat pocket, inside. See you in the morning?"

Al was waiting. When they came out of the hospital there was a barrage of flash bulbs and Tess asked what on earth was going on. But Al wouldn't say. He admitted he'd already talked to the reporters. She'd read about it in the morning papers.

"You and Matt get things fixed up?" he asked as they got into the car.

Tess turned to him in wonder. "Al, how did you know?"

"I've known a long time, Tess. Foresters are an observing lot.

"In the first place you wouldn't have bothered to run away from him if you hadn't loved him. You didn't like what he was doing, what he was heading for, so you ran away to save yourself a lifetime of frustration. You were afraid if you stayed you'd marry him as he was. He's changed.

"Then his letters. At first, I thought you were

overjoyed to see me. Later I woke up to the fact I didn't rate unless I brought a letter from Matt along with me. It's all right, girl; I didn't get in too deep."

When she drove up before his hotel he waited a moment, frowning in thought. "Tess, try to cure Matt of the idea he's responsible for Decker's death. Oh, and hurry that wedding," he added more lightly. "I'd like to be best man, and I want to get to the New Hebrides while it's summer down there."

Tess didn't stop to run a tub when she reached her room. She sank immediately into a chair and opened the long envelope.

Out fell three photographs, photographs of houses, one under construction, one just completed and one with evidence it had been lived in. Clipped to them was a note:

"Would any of these appeal to you? They're all within our bracket."

Then Matt had planned to bring these to her. It was his way of showing he'd been cured of his desire for the big Palmer house. It was

Matt's way of saying he loved her.

Tess read the morning newspapers while she was in a beauty shop having, she said, "her head repaired."

The Decker Monrove story covered the front page. There were photographs of Matt being taken from the ambulance, photographs of Mona Monrove, a photograph of Tess coming from the hospital.

There was one photograph she avoided. That was of a crumpled figure at the foot of a cliff.

Matt Seares was a hero. He'd tried to save lives by going, unarmed, to the escaped convict, pleading with him to give up without violence. He had been shot as a reward.

But he had his reward, Tess mused, and this time in a way he hadn't planned. By a completely selfless act he had gained more public recognition than he would have had by years of planned publicity.

Little was said of the lookout lady, and Tess was glad. She'd proven the safety of the towers, but there was no point in jeopardizing the peace of mind of other lookouts.

She had been referred to only as, "The fiancée

of Matt Seares, Tess Palmer, daughter of the late Judge Paulus Palmer, rushed back from a mountain vacation."

A very different-looking fiancée called upon Matt Seares the next visiting period.

"Don't I look better?" she asked. "New hair style, new clothes—"

"You look mighty nice," he conceded, "but I like this photograph in the paper even better. It says here you are my fiancée—"

"Al told them that," Tess interposed.

She repeated what King had said the night before, and he nodded. "Maybe I should plan to spend more time in the woods. Seems to give men wider vision."

They talked then about the houses, and Tess said she'd like the unfinished one, "so we can plan the interior exactly as we want it. Matt, I've never lived any place where I've done the planning. I've always had to adapt."

"That one costs less than the others," he began. "Tess, I won't be making as much in the future as I did in the past."

She laughed. "Don't worry about the grocery bills. After the careful planning I did this summer, that's one place we can economize."

They talked of other serious matters. She told him what King had said about his responsibility in Decker's death.

Finally, as their visiting time was drawing to a close, he spoke earnestly. "I've spent years gearing my ambition to one goal. I'm not promising to change everything overnight. I'll probably get busy with the boys and forget to come home to dinner. I'll plunge into some case I know I can lick, regardless of its virtues—"

"And," Tess interrupted, "when you swing too far away from the vision the Decker Monrove case has given you, I'll take off for the farthest fire district and apply for an opening as—"

"A lady lookout," they sang in unison.